The Tale of Toby Singletree

A Novel By

B. Freeman Gill

AJR
PUB
LICATIONS

www.austinjamesrobinson.org

Cover design by Mackenzie Burrows
& Kristen Michelle Keefer

First published on August 12th, 2017

ISBN:
978-0-9992029-2-0

For more information about formatting, editing, and publishing, please contact:
Austin James Robinson
+1 (325) 998-0115
austinjamesrobinson@austinjamesrobinson.org

DEDICATION

In grateful recognition of those who encouraged the writing of this book. My daughter, Savannah Gill; my sister, Eunice Choate; and my fourth graders from Sands ISD back in 1991. Then there were the pushers. A Christian brother always wanting to know: "How's the book coming along?" Louie Blount. The dear sister in Montana, Birdie Church, who cleaned one end of the table for me and said, "Sit! Write!"

And then the nagger, Patsy Zant, who sent all kinds of things in the mail. This was my favorite...

The Book

There once was a lady
Named Billie Ruth
(These facts I assure you
Are quite the truth.)
Who, so filled with prose
From her toes to her head
Inspired by the novels
She daily had read.
Said with great passion
To all those in sight
"My soul is on fire
And a book I must write."
A mystery? A thriller?
Pure fiction? Hard fact?
Of topics to choose from
There was certainly no lack.
Let the hero be handsome?
Or just honest and plain?
He could be real macho,
All brawn and no brain.
When the heroine falls
Into his arms with a sigh
Should he be embarrassed?
An "Ah, shucks," kind of guy?
The ending, so chilling,
She already knew.
But how to begin it?
She hadn't a clue.
At last it came to her
Such a _fine_ line.
In triumph she started:
"Once upon a time…"

8-10-1992
Patsy Zant

Enjoy.

PROLOGUE

It was just the nature of things. The mountains had come first. He could almost see the struggle of birth, the pain as they ripped open the earth to be born. In infancy they had been rugged and sharp. But now, as in most cases of age, they were mellowed. The beautiful mountains had worn, smooth and rounded with time. Like most forms of life, the mountains had stood the demands of wind and rain only to become stronger and more dependable.

As the young man's spirit moved to and fro, he could see there were still caves, and canyons, and great mysterious waterfalls. There was an abundance of forest, streams, and wild animals. Toby could name all of the flora and the animals. Well maybe not by the scientific names the teachers at school mentioned, but he knew what they were and what their jobs were.

Toby loved these mountains. He knew every valley and canyon as well as he knew the fine lines and wrinkles of Great Pa's face and hands. To Toby they were as one – the mountains and Great Pa. Great Pa always said he was as old as the hills. And like them, he was wise in the ways of nature. He also knew many secrets of both land and man.

Snap! Toby froze. It would have been hard to detect movement before, but now he stopped breathing. There was no movement to the eye. Toby became as the tree he leaned upon. Slowly and cautiously a doe appeared and looked about. At her heels was a small fawn. Toby breathed out slowly, and the deer took no notice of him as she led her young to water.

Seeing the mother with her fawn reminded Toby of the story of the first of his line to come to these dear mountains. He was a young Seneca Indian. They called him Runs Like A Horse. Runs Like A Horse was so named because he was very fast on his feet. He could outrun anyone who dared challenge him in the tribe and a few of their horses before he became a warrior.

But even more than his gift of running, Runs Like A Horse had "sight." He could see vision from the early age of four. His sight included the ability to read people and feel their thoughts. He accepted these gifts with innocence and dignity.

As is true in many tribes, the Shaman has great influence on the beliefs and superstitions of the people. He began to use the child's abilities as soon as he discovered them, but credited himself for all of the outcomes.

The Shaman kept 'Light Eyes', the name given to Runs Like A Horse when he was born, nearby all the time. He pretended the child had a weakness because he was born with little color in his eyes.

The tribe was getting ready for a hunt in order to be supplied for the winter camp. The hunt had been delayed because the Shaman had not told them the direction to hunt.

None of the Shaman's bag of tricks – or medicine, as he referred to it, – had given him a clue as to where to hunt. So he remembered Light Eyes. The Shaman sent for the boy. The Shaman assumed the visions would come sooner with the aid of herbal tea. As he prepared the concoction to give the boy, Light Eyes looked on.

Suddenly Light Eyes spoke. "Why do you need me to tell you where the buffalo are? Is your medicine not strong enough yet? Will I get to be a Shaman like you if I tell you where they are?"

This angered the Shaman. "What do you mean is my medicine not strong enough yet?"

"I have known a long time how you use my vision, but I have said nothing, for I also know what you will do to me if I tell."

Now this shook the Shaman, for he didn't realize the extent of the boy's sight. With anger and malice he moved toward Light Eyes. With great force he spat out, "No one will believe you. I am the Shaman. You are a weak-eyed, sick child. The child of a squaw alone. Do not challenge me."

"The buffalo are on the plain near a stream to the west," he cried as he tore away and ran for his own tepee and the tenderness of his mother.

This was the pattern for the next three or four years. Light Eyes let the Shaman use his skills while he used the Shaman for protection of his mother and their tepee. His mother did favors for those of the camp in exchange for food, but they only barely stayed alive.

Then the boy became interested in racing everything that came in sight. He could catch up to the deer. He could outrun all the young men. Soon, he was urged to challenge the young warriors for wagers. He made many warriors richer when they had tribal gatherings. He was talked about throughout the Nation as the boy who runs like a horse.

When he was about 17-years-old, he went on a name-seeking venture. He went on a journey from home. He fasted for three days and climbed into a cave to meditate.

He returned to camp seven days later. The feast was prepared by his mother, using the large deer he had brought back tied to two branches and drug in by his own power. He had no bow with which to kill, and the people gathered around and wondered.

That night at the feast, he sat between the Chief and the Shaman. When all had eaten their fill and the Chief and the Shaman had been given a gift of deer meat, Light Eyes rose before all to tell his story.

"As I lay inside the cave provided by Mother Earth, I was very light-headed and seemed to drift high above my own body. I floated outside the cave and I seemed to come to myself down in the floor of the canyon. As I stood waiting, I heard thunder and the earth shook. When I looked behind myself, I saw a great cloud of dust. Then I heard the whinnies. There coming around the bend of the canyon were many horses. I started running. I ran very hard and very fast. I must have run through several bends of the canyon wall before there was any protection. There hanging across the canyon was a tree growing out the side of the canyon wall. I leapt high and caught a branch. I had outrun the horses. Not only that but I had run as a horse for many turns in the canyon. When I returned to myself, I was in the canyon. I saw a rabbit caught by the foot in a briar bush. I prepared it and ate it. I pondered my vision. It has come to me that I must have a new name. From this day forward, I will be called 'Runs Like A Horse'.

The Shaman rose and said, "That is a warrior's name. What deed have you done to deserve to be called a warrior's name?"

"As I traveled home, I saw in my mind where a deer lay. I went to her thicket. She hurried away. I entered her sleeping place and rolled in her scent. Then I was able to get close enough to the buck that I killed him without him smelling me. I can prove this because we all ate this at the feast and you have some as a gift."

"And what warrior's bow did you use?"

The young boy grimly placed his hand on the knife at his side. "I used the blade of my father that my mother gave me for skinning! I walked near enough to grab the antlers. I pulled his head back and cut his throat. I am very fast!"

The people grinned and nudged each other all the while nodding their heads in approval.

The Shaman saw the people's approval and grunted negatively. He was about to give his answer to Light Eyes' request. The young lad knew it would not be good. Before the old medicine man could speak, Light Eyes held up his hand in a signal to wait. The Shaman waited with a scowl on his face.

"Long have I waited for a warrior's name or any name that would say who I am or what I do. I know I and my mother have been dependent on you for our food and shelter. But now I am a man. I no longer need to visit the Shaman every day – I can use my own mind. I am a man now, and I can use my own thoughts."

The others dsdid not understand, but the Shaman knew he was being challenged.

"Not only can I take care of myself and my mother, but I have brought a gift for the tribe. Out in the canyon with no way out, my brothers, you will find many horses. They are the horses of my dream and I have captured them for you. After my naming ceremony I will lead you to them."

The Shaman needed to save face. He

knew the people would be angry if he did not give his permission. If he gave the boy his name, perhaps he would still share his thoughts. However, if he did not do so, the people would be angry and there would be no telling what trail the boy's defiance would take.

The Shaman reached out his hand and put it on the young man's shoulder. "'Light Eyes' you have been called because when we look into your eyes, there is no darkness. It is as though we look straight into your other self, but from this day you shall be called 'Runs Like A Horse' as your vision has directed. And you will dwell with the warriors, as your deeds have earned the manhood. You must take care of your mother and share with the tribe." Then he painted the face and body of Runs Like A Horse with peaceable signs.

This should have been a peaceful and happy time for Runs Like A Horse, but because of his gift, he lived in fear of the Shaman. The stronger he became physically, the more control the Shaman tried to have over him. He began to threaten Runs Like A Horse with danger to his mother. The Shaman kept her under his control with spells and threats.

This was more than Runs Like A Horse

could stand. One night while the Shaman and some others had been away from camp for a few days, Runs Like A Horse went to visit his mother. She loved him very much and was delighted. She fed him and then sat near him in front of the fire.

"Mother, I must speak things to you that may not be spoken of to anyone. Your life and my life depend on you not speaking of these things. These are things only the men speak of so you may never tell the Shaman you know."

"You are very serious, my son. I trust your judgment. You have been a good son. I will honor your wishes. I will drink no more of the Shaman's tea because it makes me speak out in my sleep. I think someone listens outside of my tent."

This both surprised and alarmed the young warrior. He dashed out of the tepee and hurried into the trees nearby. He blended in immediately. He didn't wait long before he saw a young girl creeping around behind the tepee.

Runs Like A Horse crept near enough to grab ahold of her, but he did not touch her. Very gently, as though to teach not scold, he said, "Little Quail, why do you lean so near my mother's tepee? Do you not know this is considered rude? My mother would be very insulted if she knew!"

"Oh, please, please don't tell her. She is a very beautiful lady and I would not offend her. I only do it to please the Shaman. He gives me blue stones if I listen to Moon Willow speak at night."

"If I tell you where to find many such stones and others as well, will you stop being rude to my mother?"

"Yes! Yes!" she giggled.

So Runs Like A Horse told Little Quail about a stream a little way from their dwelling water.

He returned to his mother's dwelling. "How did you know it would be a child?"

"Because all that are left in the camp are people of importance. They would not do so rude a thing. Anyway I know how the Shaman uses children."

"What do you mean by that?"

"That is part of what I came to speak to you about. Now come sit near me and I will tell you a great secret."

As Runs Like A Horse began his story, the first cool breezes of autumn began to flick the leaves from their trees.

"Mother, the Shaman told me that the gods have given me a way to see what will happen in the days that are not here. He says it is because of the color of my eyes. He says someday I will go blind. He says I must tell him what I see and that others will not fear me. Now here is the part he does not know. I can also feel what others think. I have never told him that part of my gift."

"Why not, my son?"

"When I am near him I can feel his hateful thoughts for me. He would like to have me dead, but he fears my gift and needs me at the same time. Since I have become a warrior I have told him less and less about my visions."

"You could be a Shaman or a Chief yourself."

"No, kind mother, this is not my vision."

"Then what will you do, my son?"

"Mother, I have had a vision. I must leave here. Leave this tribe."

"No! You must not leave the tribe! You must not leave me! What will I do? I am too old to get a husband! You were the child of my old age. Please, Runs Like A Horse, do not leave me. I have seen 47 winters. I will not survive this one without you!"

"Mother, do you trust me?"

"Yes, of course I do. Even though you are young, you are strong and wise."

"Then listen, please. I would not leave you. I could not." He raised his hand for silence as she tried to protest. "I can see what will happen. I have been shown already. We – you and I – will travel south. We will cross many rivers and climb many mountains. This will be a very white winter here, but not in the south so much. No, no, no, now listen. We must leave tomorrow night. That is the last chance before the moon starts its growth. You know that when the scouting party returns, the Shaman will not let me go."

"We can not be ready so soon. There are so many preparations for such a journey," insisted his mother.

"No, mother. Get your most treasured things for me tonight. I have a hiding place for them. Tomorrow after the sun begins to fall to the resting place, but before dark, we will go for a stroll. The people will not know we are leaving. We will take only two horses that I have already put in a hiding place. You will ride one and the other will carry your hides and two blankets. Only two."

And so Runs Like A Horse made a few trips that night to make preparations to leave the next afternoon.

The next afternoon he came to his mother's tepee and made sure he was seen entering. Sometime later he did just the opposite. He sent his mother out as though she were answering the call of nature while he waited in her home. Then at just the right time, he left her tepee unnoticed. They would not be missed for a long time. They were believed to be in the tepee or out walking.

Runs Like A Horse put his mother's white buffalo robe – the one on which he was born – and the great grizzly's skin on a sturdy looking roan mare. Then he helped his mother up on the horse's back. He tied her other things and two baskets onto the other horse with leather strips.

He held onto the reins of the pack-horse and led it away from the home he had known for 17 years. Sure of his visions without fear for the future, he traveled for ten months and brought his mother to the Smokey Mountains to live.

CHAPTER 1

Toby was so deep in thought that he didn't hear his great-grandfather's approach.

"Ho! There you are. Did I disturb your dreams?"

"No, Great Pa. Good morning. I was only remembering your father and grandmother. The deer I watched reminded me of what great care they took of each other and how I've come to be here."

"Yes. My father had a great gift and I think sometimes I see it in you."

"No, Great Pa. I have a spirit that comes to me sometimes, but I cannot understand what it says."

"Maybe in time, Toby. You are young."

"I'm not sure I want to know what others think, or to look into the future."

"Then maybe you should not seek the gift."

"I am content to have the spirit of the

animals and be able to become one with the trees."

"That is where you got your name. You hid in the forest one day from a roaming bear. He couldn't pick you out as one single tree from the others. So your father called you 'Little Single Tree'."

"Yes, but my dear mother called me Toby."

"You should be careful not to speak of the dead. It is not right. You might call the spirit back and cause it to be caught between two worlds forever."

"Yes, I know, Great Pa, but the last thing my mother said to me was, 'Remember me always'. Maybe because she was white, she felt different. Anyway, the white people below talk about their dead all the time."

"This could be true. They do, don't they? Anyway, speak carefully."

"Yes, Great Pa."

They stopped talking and started walking back toward their home. There was always a contest between the two. They would see who could go through the forest traveling new trails side-by-side without disturbing the floor of the forest or making a sound the other would hear.

This little game began when Toby was a

very small boy. It was the way his great-grandfather first started teaching him the way to move through his world without detection.

As they silently walked, Toby began to think about the time he first showed up at the store in the lowland.

No one knew where he came from or whose child he was. He just came down the mountain trail that day holding tightly to the gnarled old hand of his great-grandfather. He was a child of many auras. He was strong. From his eyes came a dual look of wisdom and charity. His laughter rippled like a stream flowing over pebbles. There was sweetness and strength in his manner. The old recluse Indian leant mystery to the boy's presence.

They approached the old log building with purpose and intent in their steps. It was amazing how the old building had stood the passing of years. It had been home for some early settlers, used as shelter for wayfaring strangers, hideout for many endangered two-legged species, and government Trading Post to promote trade between the whites and some long ago Indians.

That is probably why they called it The Post now. It was a long, wide building built on a wooden floor. It contained tables and shelves piled high with all kinds of goods that mountain folk might need. There was a big pot-bellied stove in the center where the old men gathered in bad weather to speculate on the future and to solve all the world problems as they spat tobacco juice and carved on wood. On the good weather days, they did these same chores on the great long porch that fronted the building, or they sat on the fallen logs under the trees that naturally landscaped the area.

It was as if time stood still in the backwoods of these mountains. These folks still lived the same way their folks did before them.

Only the bright expression that came to Toby's face showed that the men had been acknowledged. No word was spoken as the giant of a man walked across the way, stepped upon the porch, and stooped over to enter the six-foot door. Toby silently followed.

"Good morning, Moses."

"Otson."

"Who's ya partner?"

"Mr. Otson, Toby Little Single Tree, my great-grandson."

"Toby went straight to the store-keeper with his hand extended and an open smile on his face. Otson was surprised.

This young man had the strength and

countenance of an Indian, and the poise and charm of a white man. This was the first he, or anyone for that matter, ever heard of old Moses having any kin. All on the mountain thought of him as one who lived alone in an old cabin built right up against a mountainside. He came to The Post occasionally to trade for coffee and flour or meal.

"Well, Toby, where did you come from, and how long have you been with old Samson?" The young children who knew the Bible story called him that because he was so big and his hair was so long.

The boy was not allowed to answer Mr. Otson. Moses called him to the part of the store where the shoes were piled on a table against one wall.

"Great Pa, do I have to have these kinds of shoes? I want some like yours. Your kind don't make funny noises or choke my legs the way these do. 'Sides, I can't get close to the deer when I wear the hard kind of shoes."

"You speak truth about white man's shoes," smile Great Pa. "You have decided. Come."

The proprietor could hardly contain his curiosity. He was not alone. Those who were sitting about spitting and whittling had entered the building on one pretext or the other.

The old man now added tobacco and stick candy to his other items.

Proprietor Otson totaled the supplies. Toby watched the candy eagerly. His great-grandfather handed him a piece of it. Toby smiled and started out the door.

"Now, son, are you sure I can't sell you a new pair of shoes?" asked Otson.

Toby turned in the door and very solemnly spoke, "I have said!"

Moses paid with a few coins from his pouch, gathered his goods, then walked out of The Post. He smiled knowingly and took his secrets with him.

Toby and Great Pa walked as one through the mountain's forest. Moses had lived 87 years in these mountains. He was born before the white man's great war with each other. The mountains had seen him grow from infancy to man. He was as tall and strong as the grand trees in the forest. His roots were planted deep and, like the young saplings, he could bend and spring back in the storms of life he faced.

Toby reached over for his great-grandfather's arm as he came back from his reminiscence. They walked along secure in each other's presence.

"Great Pa, I was just recalling my first visit to The Post, and I remembered a question Otson asked me. You called me to you very quickly when he asked where I had come from. Why was I not allowed to answer Mr. Otson's question?"

"It is best, Toby, to keep a white man confused! The less he knows, the more he wonders. The more he wonders, the less he knows. That is confusing to the mountain white man."

"Do you also remember when you and I went to the Smitty's soon after? The day you met your friends."

"You were pretty impressive even at the age of five. You sure kept folks wondering. The folks that lived in the village watched amused as you tried to walk in my footprints that were left in the snow. You wore some bearskin leggings. You would say to anyone who asked about them, 'Ole bruther bear loant 'em to me for the winter'."

"Sure, I remember. That's the day I got my first dog. You were in with the Smitty. I played outside. I threw some crumbs to the chickens in the yard. There was a dog yelping around the building so I went around to see what was happening. Some big guys were stoning an old strut dog."

"Hey, I got 'em!"

"No, I did. That was my throw!"

"Well, watch this."

"I ran between the dog and the boy, and said, 'Don't hit my dog, please!'"

"Ain't chure dawg," one shouted.

"I asked, 'Is he yours?'"

"No, he ain't nobody's," was the retort.

"Then he's mine, I told them. I called that ole red dog, and he followed me back to the entrance of the Smitty's."

That had indeed been an introduction to a strange relationship. Those five cousins were the town bullies. They were nearly always up to no good. They were the young'uns from the O'Shira Clan. Three brothers came from Ireland a couple of generations back and the boys were the offspring. They ranged in age from seven to twelve. What they wanted they either took by force, outnumbered the foe, or overcame by sheer audacity.

They couldn't believe what had just happened. One boy had interfered. One kid. Just one kid? And alone! Who was he?

They glanced at one another, and silently agreed to take him on. All of them at once. They began to pelt Toby and the dog with rocks.

Now, Toby knew no fear. He walked toward the boys and started dodging the rocks. The big red dog snarled and stood by the boy's side.

The boys were beginning to slow down as they ran out of the stones they had gathered. They stood there glaring at him. About the time they had decided to jump on Toby and risk the dog, Moses came out of the Smitty's door. He was an Indian who had grown up in these mountains, and he was one mountain of a man. He must have looked like a bear to the young rascals.

At any rate, when he growled really big, they all turned tail and ran in five different directions. Moses roared with laughter.

"Well, now what have we here? Where did you find your new friend?"

"He didn't belong to nobody so I took him, Great Pa."

"Well, we best be gitten' on back up the mountain 'fore it gits too cold, boy. Bring your friend along."

And they continued working their memories as they silently walked through the forest.

CHAPTER 2

In those days back in the hills of the Smokey Mountains near the Chattahoochee River, those poor mountain folk talked – if they talked at all – about their problems with the revenuers and the uppity flatlanders when they got together.

These people did not live in the dark ages, but neither did they know much of the modern conveniences. They lived like their parents had lived generation after generation. A few who lived lower in the hills had old pickup trucks. Many still used a hand plow in their gardens. If they were lucky enough to have a mule, they might plant a few extra acres of corn.

They had at least two pigs that raised a litter every year. This gave them food and a little money. They had chickens and, of course, several of them had stills hidden in the forest of the hills.

It didn't matter what age the stranger was; the hill people didn't open up to outsiders.

Toby's father had grown up in these hills, but he never did fit in. He never wanted to go to school. He didn't make friends easily. All his young life, he longed to go away. He spoke to all of the city people that would talk to him.

After they received word from the War Department that his father had been killed in the war, he was even more restless. He went to his grandfather and spoke his heart. He spoke of his dream to live in the white man's modern city, to have a house where the water came inside, and, most of all, to drive one of the cars the city people drove.

Tobias left soon after that in 1926. He went to find a more exciting life. No one heard from him or knew where he had gone.

Ten years later, a stranger appeared at the door of the small cabin built up against the mountainside. A frail, young woman carried a big-eyed three-year-old and a letter from the runaway.

Great Pa took the child in; he read the letter. Then he put Toby's history away until he was old enough to handle the information, and began to care for the woman and child.

CHAPTER 3

Toby was a very sweet and accepting child. He was very opposite from his restless father. From the beginning, he loved Great Pa. He was obedient and eager to learn. His natural curiosity kept his great-grandfather always on the move.

The first thing he learned was the secret of the one-roomed cabin. At the back of the cabin was a wall that had what looked like a four foot set-in. It had wooden stubs in various places. Different things were hanging from them. It appeared to be a niche for storage.

In truth, it was a sliding door. Toby found it while playing with the stubs. Behind the door was a great dark hold. Right away, Toby ran to get Great Pa to show him his discovery. "Look, Great Pa, we must fill in the big hold. A bear might come in and sometimes I hear things." Toby had told his mother he heard talking coming from the back wall, but she laughed and told him to go play.

"No, Toby, you may hear echoes of the past. Do not fear. This is the way I built this cabin. Behind is a large cave. It is the cave of your great-great-grandfather. It is where I was born. They do not need to know everything. When you are older, I will take you inside the cave. Until I do, you must not mention this to anyone."

But Toby was introduced to the cave much sooner than was planned. Toby's mother, whom his father had called Yellow Flower, died a few weeks after their arrival. She had suffered much with the coughing of lung disease. She had lived too long in the slum area of a polluted factory-laden city.

Great Pa had taken limbs of trees into the cave. There he built a burial place on top of the ground. It was placed deep in the cave. He wrapped her body in her blanket and laid it on the pyre. He put bear grease on her body and set a fire to it.

As the burning ritual of his mother took place, young Toby let his eye wander over the cave. On the walls were strange drawings. It was a beautiful place. Down near the back was a pool of clear water. Toby thought he heard a great constant roar, but he decided it must be the fire. He stared at the fire, and a tear trickled down his face.

That was the last time Toby went into the cave for several years. His great-grandfather did what he could to help him to accept the death of his mother.

He explained how death must come to help bring forth new life. He explained by using the corn seed and the stalk of corn. But it bothered Toby when Great Pa told him not to mention the dead by name. Toby wanted to talk not only of his mother, but also of his father.

Great Pa stood firm. So Toby spoke to the animals, the trees, and the sun, moon, and stars about his losses. Toby became very close to nature.

CHAPTER 4

When Toby was seven-years-old, he saw the other children going into a small building and not coming out. He went into The Post where his great-grandfather was making a purchase. "Great Pa, why do the young'uns go into that building?"

Otson walked over to the lad and put his hand on the boy's shoulder. Then answering for Great Pa, he said, "Why that's the school. We're proud of that school. True, you can't go to one of them universities from it, but you can learn to read n' spell n' a good deal about numbers. And you can go to the flatland school knowin' what you learn from this school."

"Can I go to that school, Great Pa?"

Once again, Otson answered before Great Pa could. "Now, Toby, I'm not sure they'll let an Indian go to school."

Great Pa stepped between Otson and

Toby. "You want to go there, Toby?"

"Yes, Great Pa."

"Then come. You will go. I know the man who teaches the little ones."

So they left and went down the road to the school. To Toby's great pleasure, the man greeted Great Pa with outstretched hands. Great Pa spoke to him for a few minutes. When he walked away, Great Pa smiled down at Toby. "Well, we need to go back to The Post. I need to get you a slate and some chalk to use to learn to write with."

The next day, Toby was up early to get ready for school.

"Toby, there's something I must tell you. The children may tease you. They may call you Injin or they may call you breed, or half-breed. Do not let this stop what you want. The important thing is to use this school to teach your needs, not to let some wicked child turn your head from your goals. There will always be some white man who tries to tromp you down. You are Toby Little Single Tree. No one can get past that!"

"Yes, Great Pa. I do this for myself and because my mother wanted me to go to school."

"When you are old enough and can read the white man's letters, there is something I will give you that was left in my care for when you are ready."

"What is it, Great Pa?"

"No more about it now. I was told to wait until I thought you were ready."

"Yes, Great Pa. I will go to school now."

"No, wait. Today I will take you to school in the truck." Now, Great Pa had a very unique vehicle. He had found an old rusted-out horseless carriage. The motor had been disposed of. He took the tires and cleared them down to the wheel. Then he built an extension onto the back and made it look more like a buckboard.

It even had a socket for a whip! This was convenient because Great Pa hooked the carriage up to his old plow horse. Everyone in the mountains talked about the carriage and called it 'Moses' truck'. It gave him great prestige. The mountain people all admired Moses because of his strength and honesty, as well.

"Wow, Great Pa, why do you do this?"

"It is time. The people need to know the importance I place on you getting to go to a school to learn. It is time to learn as much of the white man's world as you can. Your white ancestors must be honored as well as your Indian ones."

Toby hugged his great-grandfather around the knees. "I love you, Great Pa."

And they went to school. The horse and horseless carriage wound down the trail to the village.

The old men at The Post stood, took off their caps, scratched their heads, and grinned their toothless grins. Toby arrived for his first day of school in great style. Great Pa let him crawl down by himself and said, "I'll be at The Post at 3 o'clock when you get out."

"Yes, Great Pa."

Toby took his slate and chalk, along with his lunch bucket, and went into the schoolhouse.

Mr. Macon met him at the door. The other children were settling down to work at their desk. Mr. Macon took Toby's slate and asked, "And what is your name, young man?" He poised his chalk in waiting above the slate.

Toby didn't want to refer to himself as Little Single Tree, but he wanted to honor both of his parents' names for him. So he took a deep breath and said, "I am Toby Single Tree."

The teacher wrote on his slate, "Toby Singletree." He also made some numbers and handed the slate back to Toby. "Take this and copy your name and these numbers over and over again until you can write them. Go sit in that seat up front."

Toby took his seat and looked around at the others in the row. They were tracing around the letters and numbers before trying on their own. Toby tried the method. He got the feel for it. It was like drawing. He did it. He did it. And in no time at all, he could write his name.

CHAPTER 5

The first few days went by without a hitch. Great Pa even accepted Toby's new way to say his name.

The O'Shira boys were not rejecting Toby's presence, but neither had they acknowledged it. They just ignored him. They had decided they weren't ready to maybe tangle with the old Indian. They had not yet become that bold. So to get hold of Toby, they had to wait until he was allowed to go home from school alone.

Of course what they misunderstood were the old Indian's motives for coming for Toby in the afternoons. Great Pa just liked being with his great-grandson. He didn't come to protect his little grandson as they had believed. At seven, going on eight, Toby was already quite a tracker and most reliable in the forest, especially so on his side of the mountains. He was also a pretty fair wrestler.

And so, even as other adults in the area, Moses finally gave up his afternoons with Toby to go about his chores and other work. Toby began to come to school alone and to return home alone.

After a few days of observing the new habit of Toby going home alone, the cousins decided to follow him home.

They had not forgotten the time he had rescued the big red dog. Just him all alone had ruined their fun with the dog.

They were hardly a mile from school and Toby was certain he was being followed. Toby didn't know what was going on, but he wanted to find out before he went home. So he led his followers away in another direction.

He headed out straight as he could go to an old deserted shack. He went in the door as though he lived there. Toby went directly to the back window, climbed out, and circled the old house from behind to a large tree. He was up the tree and stretched out on a branch like a panther before the followers were hidden well behind the trees outside the cleared area near the old house.

Toby watched. Soon the boys signaled each other and withdrew. They were satisfied. Toby had gone home, and they had followed him undetected.

"See, I told you we could do it." This was from Ezekiel, the oldest.

His younger brother, Daniel (they were both named after prophets from the Bible), observed, "Wonder where the old silly looking truck is."

"The old Injin is gone with it, Dummy!"

Toby came down from the tree as the boys moved quietly back down the trail plotting their ambush. He continued his journey home.

When Toby arrived, Great Pa was placing small sticks under the cooking pot. They greeted one another, and Great Pa stepped inside the tepee that was set up a few feet from the small log cabin.

They used the tepee while the weather permitted. Great Pa didn't like what the cold weather did to his old joints and bones, so he spent bad weather days and cold seasons in the log cabin with the fire roaring hot.

As Great Pa came back out of the tepee with their evening meal, he asked, "Well, how is the world of school? Are you still wanting to go?"

"Yes, Great Pa, I like it. I still want to go. The O'Shira young'uns even played a little game of trail following today after school. We may play some more another day. So don't worry if I'm late a few afternoons."

"Ah, Toby, the spirits are your guide. I never worry about you. Now tell me about your lessons."

"Great Pa, I have a lot of fun with the numbers. I can make the letters and say the sounds. But I don't know how to make the words speak."

"And can all the other children make the words speak?"

"Not all. But some. They all have seen more winters than me. That is except Clyde and Mossie. Oh yeah, I like the music time too. I like it when Mr. Macon makes the music way down low. It makes my inerds rumble. I like to sing too. But you know what? I don't like to do it all together. There's too much noise. I can't hear us sing."

"I'll have to come and hear you sometime."

"Come early. We do it first thing and then put our hand on our heart and make a vow!"

"What vow?"

"You know. About the flag and how we will take care of it, and fight to keep it free."

"Hmm. Like your grandpa. He died for that flag in a way that was fought. It was early in the war back in 1917."

"Tell me about it."

"Sometime. Now let's get back to these talking words," he said with an inward smile. "Tomorrow you bring some of those words home with you and we'll see if we can figure out what they say."

This made Toby very happy, and with that, he dipped into his food happily.

After school the next day, Toby was aglow with the belief that Great Pa could help him learn to read. He patted his pocket to reassure himself that he had brought his list of words.

Toby was eager to get home so he decided to run. He had run only a short way when he pulled up and stopped suddenly. He looked around and listened. Stillness. No birds chirping. No critter stirred. He decided to get off the path into the trees. As he did, he caught a movement in the rocks to his left. He eased over in that direction.

There sat Clyde trying to be still and quiet, but it just wasn't in his nature.

"Whatcha hidin' from?

"Shh! We're gonna jump a Injin."

"I'm a half Indian."

Awakening came slowly to Clyde. "Granny's drawers! Toby, you ain't s'posed to be here. You're s'posed to be hidin' or getting away!"

"Aw, I don't have time to play today. Tell Zeek some other day, I gotta get home early."

So now he knew. But it didn't bother him. After this, he'd be more cautious. He headed out like he was going to the shack of yesterday's game. It wasn't long before he dashed off in the direction of home.

When he arrived, he was surprised to see what looked like a stack of something with a deer hide thrown over it. "What's under the hide, Great pa?"

"You tell me."

"Oh boy, another tracking lesson. I haven't had one of those for awhile."

"That's because I thought you had learned. But it seems you need to be reminded of an important lesson. Now, you have seen there is something under the skin. Go up into the tree and look down on it."

Like a flash, Toby was up the tree and out on the branch leaning over the skin. Great Pa removed the skin.

"Why Great Pa, this isn't hard. That looks like a pile of little tree branches."

"So it does, but what is it?"

Toby backed off the branch and down the tree slowly as he looked at the little logs. "From one side it still looks like a pile of wood, but the other side has a hole cut in it. A window! You've made a log cabin!"

"Have I now? Did you observe all tracks before you decided what animal it is?"

"No."

"Must you?"

"Yes, or I won't have the whole."

"So?"

"I'll look at the side I have not yet seen."

When Toby walked around to the back of the small log cabin, he was surprised. "Oh look, Great Pa. It has been burned. It also has small bits of rock stuck to it with red clay."

"So now tell me, what is it?"

"I would say it was the toy of a small girl. Made for her by someone who loved her. Look at the little rooms and steps up to them. When it caught on fire, someone threw it into the river to put out the fire. The current probably took it before it could be reclaimed. It floated down and into the little stream of red clay. You found it; brought it here to teach me a great lesson."

"A lesson, Toby, not just in tracking, but also your reading. I know you are puzzled, but let me explain. You see, many times when we are tracking we study the track and not the trail. It is easy to say, 'Oh, it's the track of a bear'. But is it a friendly bear? Is he hunting? Is he hurt? Does he seek revenge? Is it a he?

We need to know the whole story before we let the bear see us. I think it is the same with your reading."

"How, Great Pa?"

"Let me see your list of words you brought."

Great Pa wrote on the ground.

"Now what did I write?"

"Sss, mm, o, kk, and the e doesn't have a sound at the end of a word."

"Now, Toby, the way I see it: this word is the track of an animal. To figure which animal, you must take all parts of the track and put them together. The sound makes the impression in your head like an animal would on the ground. Now, don't take each sound separately, but let them blend together softly like the grains of sand."

So Toby tried again, "Ssmmokk." He listened. "Smoke." A light on his face. "Smoke," he said. "Tree, tree! Hat, nose. I can do it, Great Pa, I can do it! Let's go to school now and show Mr. Macon. He'll be so glad."

Great Pa smiled with great pride, "I think he would rather we wait until tomorrow. But you can read your list to me and be ready for tomorrow."

So with great exultation, he read and reread all of his words and found he could walk around his house and read all of the written words there. He could hardly wait for school the next day.

The next day, Toby was off and running bright and early, calling back over his shoulder, "I'll be late. I'll play the game with the O'Shira boys."

Great Pa watched as Toby disappeared into the forest. He couldn't help but wonder what game the boys were so intent upon. Had he known, he would have pitied the O'Shira cousins because he would have known that Toby was ruthless in the forest when it came to protecting the animals. Today they would find out for themselves.

CHAPTER 6

When Mr. Macon asked for a reader, Toby raised his hand at once. "You, Toby?" he asked in surprise.

"I've learned to make the letters speak, Mr. Macon."

"And how did that happen?" Mr. Macon was aglow. "Now, Toby, you must tell us how this happened."

"Well," began Toby, "Great Pa made me see how reading is like tracking. You must study the prints then you look at the whole thing by softly blending the clues together, and then they talk to you." Toby was breathless and excited.

"Big deal," said Ezekiel unimpressed. "I've been reading for three years."

"Yes, Zeek, but you've been in school for five years. Toby has only been here this year. And I'm very pleased with how well you both read."

Because of his newfound understanding, Toby realized how much easier all of the other schoolwork is. The day passed quickly, and school was soon out.

"And now the game," thought Toby. He was glad that he had seen Clyde the day before and the game was unintentionally revealed to him.

He immediately took off for the trail to the old deserted cabin. Then he very deliberately left a good solid trail as he veered off to the left toward the river. He knew all the boys could swim; he'd seen them. The water was only a little chilled so off he went to play "the game."

By the time the boys stepped out of the forest onto the rocky beach, Toby was several feet out into the water.

"Hey, y'all! Come on and swim."

"Whatcha doing in the river?" asked Clyde.

"I'm just playin' 'fore I go on home."

"You're crazy. Why ya gotcha clothes on?" This came from Zeek.

"I ain't crazy. Water's nice. 'Sides, you know Indians always use whatever they have on for whatever they are doin'. Are ya scarta come in? Dare ya to swim out as far as me. Betcha can't. I guess Indians and half Indians can just do more than plain white people," he jeered.

That was just too much. Zeek began taking his clothes off. "You gonna do it, Zeek?" asked Daniel.

"Yeah, and that ain't all. So's ever one of youins. Ya ain't gonna shame me in front of no half a Injin. Take 'em off and git in or I'll whup ya all."

So all five boys peeled off their clothes, put them on a log beside the water, and shivered and yelped out into the river. As soon as the three biggest were in far enough that they could swim, Toby went underwater and headed for the shore. He reached the shore just as Daniel looked up. He stopped swimming and started yelling, "Hey, he's already back yonder! Hey, Zeek, look at that Injin! He's stealin' our clothes!"

Zeek came out of the water spitting and gulping for air enough to yell. All three started back to the shore at once. But they were too late. By the time they got back to where the two youngest were playing in the water, Toby was at the edge of the forest waving their clothes in the air.

Zeek shoved Clyde backward into the water. "Why didn't ya stop him? Ya let 'm git our clothes."

"Granny's drawers, Zeek! We didn't even see him 'til ye yelled at me. We was playin' in the water!"

Jake looked up and saw Toby still standing at the edge of the rock beach. "We'll git cha fer this!"

"Aw, Jake, I'm just playing your game. And look," he said as he held up the clothes, "I just made a little Indian coup!"

"Let's git him!" cried Zeek.

The boys took off after Toby as fast as they cold go. They ran buck naked across the beach into the forest.

"We shore better find him. Our Pa'll skin our hides raw fer lettin' a lil' ole half breed snoocker us this a way."

Jessie, the middle boy, was grinning inside. It always pleased him when someone put the harness on Zeek or Daniel. They always thought they were so tough just cause they were older and bigger. They were always pushing him and Clyde and Jake around. Big bossy bullies. Jessie smiled to himself at the three B words. "Well, come on, let's hurry 'fore he gits plum away."

A few yards into the woods, they saw hanging from a low branch five pairs of very worn and stained, smelly pairs of homemade drawers.

Jake observed, "We shoulda wore our clothes in the water."

"Yeah," tuned in Clyde, "least they'da maybe smelled better."

"That's probly why ole Tobe didn't wanna keep um," giggled Jessie. And Jake and Clyde joined in.

"Come on, you hyenies," growled Zeek. "He's morin' likely headed home."

So they took off running between the trees and jumping the dead falls. Five boys from seven to thirteen, as wild as deer, were after one boy about seven, who had tricked them into the water and stolen their clothes.

By the time the cousins came sneaking around the last turn, Toby had spread their clothes out on the corral fence. The pants were on one level and the shirts were on another. Toby was up in a tree to observe.

The boys came into the area very carefully. Their approach was quite comical to Toby. They ran from one tree very quickly to the next tree. When they came to the clearing, Jake yelled out with glee, "There they are!"

Four sets of hands grabbed at him at once and pulled him behind a big tree. "Shh! You want the old one to come out and scalp you?"

With that, Toby nearly rolled out of his tree.

The boys scampered quickly past the cabin to the fence with their clothes. They pulled on their pants as fast as they could the whole time falling into the fence and each other. All in all it was a pretty funny sight.

Jessie started out just smiling very broadly, then he snickered, giggled, and finally fell down laughing right out loud. "Would ya look at us? We look like that bunch of circus clowns we saw down in the town one time." He continued rolling around holding his sides with tears rolling down his face. "Didn't ole Toby put it to us, oh boy, didn't he? Ya know, this has been great fun." And he continued laughing.

By this time the other four had broken down. Even Zeek was laughing. "We're gonna have to keep our eyes on him if we're gonna keep our pants."

They all laughed. With this new slant on things, Toby dropped down from the tree and joined in the merriment. No one noticed. He laughed and poked and got poked. "You shoulda seen your face, Daniel, when you saw me grab your clothes."

"Yeah! I was real surprised. Hey, where'd you come from?"

"Does it matter? We had fun, huh?" he replied.

"Yeah, we did. Maybe we could all do something together next time," said Zeek.

"I kinda thought we had done this together," grinned Toby.

With that thought, Jessie led them in another round of laughter.

"You're alright, Toby. For a kid. Not as stupid as some lil' kids I could mention."

"Why don't we go huntin' sometime? We don't have guns, but I bet you don't either."

"Nope, Great Pa says it ain't right to hunt a helpless animal with guns. 'Sides, I only hunt what I can eat."

"That's what we do," said Jessie. "If only we could kill something, we might get enough to eat."

"Well, we could do a little right now," whispered Toby. "Sit real still. Now feel around your body with just your hands. Keep your eyes still or closed. Find a good chuckin' rock. Be still. Let me tell you where to chuck. Put a picture of the cabin in your head. About the middle of the wall, between the step and the corner, is a rabbit. Shh. Don't move, but open your eyes and find the rabbit. He's smelling the air. He's raisin' up. When I say 'now', everybody chuck at him. Sh…wait, NOW."

The rocks started flying and the boys

started running and picking up rocks on the run.

"Ow! You stupid, don't hit me," yelled Daniel as someone fired one into his leg.

"Look I got'm," yelled Clyde.

"Ya didn't neither. I did," cried Jake.

They fell out on the ground fighting.

The other four took out after the rabbit. It wasn't dead, but it's back leg was broken. Toby reached into his pocket and brought out his pocketknife. He very swiftly cut the rabbit's throat and held it up by its back feet.

"I'll carry it home," said Zeek.

"Wait. Let's take the innards out. That way it won't taste funny when you eat it."

"I never heard that one," said Daniel.

"That's what Great Pa says," Toby replied.

"How come you get to carry it home, Zeek? I kilt it," said Clyde, who had finally stopped wrestling with Jake.

"No, you didn't," scowled Jake.

Before they could start at it again, Daniel joined in with Jake. He was also scowling. "How do you know who kilt it? We was all chuckin' at it. Maybe I kilt it or Jessie or Toby."

Then Toby said, "Why don't we eat it here and now; then we could all have some of it?"

"You mean go into your house?" Zeek asked doubtfully as he looked toward the cabin.

"Now, that ain't my house. I just didn't want you to go home with me that first time. I wanted to see what you was up to tracking me like ya wuz."

Once again, Jessie was alive with admiration for Toby. Chuckling as he spoke, "You mean ya knew we were trailin' ya? We shore ain't very sneaky trackers, huh, Zeek?"

"Then who lives here?" Daniel wanted to know.

"It's just a place. Nobody stays here. I think it belongs to an old friend of my grandpa."

"Well, I'm hungry! I wanna know how we can eat that rabbit now," whined Clyde, while Jake chimed his agreement.

So Toby sent them out looking for wood to burn, small branches to hang the rabbit on, and stones to place around the fire. He prepared the rabbit using the step at the house for a worktable.

Everything was ready except the fire. Toby reached into his pocket and drew out a small oiled waterproof pouch. All eyes were glued to what he was doing. He very carefully pulled out a sulfur match.

"Granny's drawers, Toby! I thought you'd have some kinda Injin magic in that ole pouch. It's just a match. Same as we use."

Toby started the fire and they all placed their green sticks with a hunk of rabbit on them across the fire. The heart of the rabbit lay on the step.

Toby said, "The real warrior eats the heart of his first kill because this gives him strength from the animal. Now who said they killed it?"

"You mean eat it raw?" queried Daniel.

"Hey! Who knows who kilt it. Isn't that what you said? Anybody coulda done it. Anyway we only broke his leg. Toby, you kilt it with your knife when ya cut his throat. Are you gonna eat that rabbit's heart?" Zeek asked.

"Naw. I ain't no warrior. And I'm jist half an Indian. The other half of me likes cooked meat."

They all laughed and ate their rabbit. This was the first of many such hunting adventures the boys had together.

The older Toby grew, the more excited he became about the mountains in which he lived. Great Pa believed in personal freedoms, and he never tried to stop Toby from exploring. He did caution him about going out of the mountains and into town where the flatlanders lived. He said they have a different law that they live by, and they didn't care too much about mountain people. He made Toby give his word to stay away until he was older and had a greater understanding.

So Toby gave his word and began to explore the land in which he lived. He already knew well the cabin area where he lived with Great Pa.

He had learned to swim in the calm pool near the bottom of the waterfall. He had learned he wasn't big enough to scale the wall of the rock cliff that was the north boundary of his home, but he vowed someday to climb to the top.

At this, Great Pa only chuckled and said, "Better goats than you have tried."

Every day when he emerged from his sleeping place, Toby would greet the great wall and carefully look over it for a means of assent. Then he would be off on his adventures.

They lived in a huge lip that branched out of the mountain at the base of the cliff. This lip was about two acres of ground before it tapered some to the last forest and fell off to another lip, which angled down into the village. This was the dirt track that Great Pa traveled with his remodeled truck.

To the west of the lip and just a little bend of the cliff was the hard working waterfall. It was fed by the Okeechobee River that ran about 20 feet northwest of the cliff. A fast moving, wide stream fed the waterfall. It had never stopped flowing in all the years Great Pa knew about and he had been born there.

Toby wondered how it didn't "just come on over" to their place.

Great Pa explained, "The river has cut a path deeper and deeper into the rocky shore and created a wall on the bank much like a dam. That holds the water in its bed. Now, you see all this good earth where we plant our corn and our garden, and how rich the soil is? Well, many years before my father came here, the river flooded many times and washed the soil over the cliff. That is why the top of the cliff is only large smooth stones, and we have about two feet of rich, fertile ground."

CHAPTER 7

"On a hill far away stood an old rugged cross. The emblem of suffering and shame." The words and tunes floated on the air through the woods. Toby heard them as he ran toward home late one evening at the end of an afternoon of fishing like the bear. He stopped to listen to the song. He could hear the voices of both men and women as the song carried clearly in the night. He very quietly walked toward the origin of the sound. Through the trees of the forest, he could see a small building. He approached and quietly sat on the hillside at the edge of the forest. He sat there and listened to the singing of several songs.

He was so completely mesmerized by the singing that he forgot where he was until suddenly one of the fish he had caught flopped on the stringer where he had laid it on the ground beside him. Toby jumped because it startled him. "Thank you, fish," he said. "I'd better get home."

When Toby arrived, Great Pa had already started a fire outside the tepee lodging. "I knew you wouldn't come back empty-handed. Everything's all ready. All we gotta do is clean 'em, cook 'em, and eat 'em," he said. "So what did you find new today on your journey?" Great Pa knew that Toby was always discovering something new about life and the wonders of his environment.

Toby told his great-grandfather about his fun afternoon trying to fish with his hands. How he had to be as still as a rock to fool the fish as they swan past his spread apart legs. Then he would put his hands slowly into the water and wait for just the right time to grab a fish. He went on and on with his funny stories until they had their fish skewered across the fire to cook.

They sat on the ground near the fire and watched the fire or the fish or both. "Great Pa, ya know that little cabin – the one that's been painted white? The one that has the words hanging over the door that says 'Church of Christ meets here'. Well I've gone past it lots of times, but this is the first time anybody was ever there."

"And what were they doing there?"

"Singing."

"Singing? Is that all?"

"That's all I heard or saw."

"Well, Toby, I know for sure that some people go there. They meet to worship God. The people I've noticed there seem to be good folks."

"I thought God was everywhere and in everything. Wonder why they go into that little house to do it."

"I just don't know why some folks do what they do. One thing I do know: these fish are ready for us to eat them and I thank our God for them."

"Me too," was the hungry reply.

Toby went to bed early that evening. He had been out on the mountain all day, and he had plans to meet and go hunting with Jessie early the next morning. He was sure glad there would be no school.

CHAPTER 8

The years had passed quickly for Toby since he first came to the mountain to live with Great Pa. He could not remember his life before Great Pa.

He could remember strutting around the fire near the cabin he shared with his mother. She always coughed and was very tired. Great Pa took care of him and his mother. She spent most of her day on a bed near the fire. Her hand seemed always to be held out to him. "Never forget me, Toby. Speak of me, if it is only to yourself. I am not a Seneca Indian, so you can speak of me. Great Pa will not understand, but you will someday. Remember me, Toby."

He remembered. Even as he played and grew, and studied, and changed, he remembered.

As the years had passed and changed, so had this – his thirteenth summer passed quickly. Zeek and Daniel had left school the year before to help their pa with the work at home. That only left Jake, Clyde, and Jessie free to hunt and fish during the summer.

One day the boys decided to go fishing once more before school started again. They scattered up and down the Chattahoochee River each trying to find the best spot. Jessie had found a place where the water seemed to slow before it tore quickly around the bend toward the old sawmill.

Clyde and Jake ran past them and jeered because they declared there was a better place up the river. Toby and Jessie paid them no heed. They found young tree limbs and built three fish traps and put them into the water. They found a nice shady willow tree to lie down under and tell each other yarns.

Jessie had caught two fish and Toby had caught only one, much to Jessie's joy. Jessie teased, "It looks like the fish like my trap better'n yourn today."

Toby was stopped from answering back by an inhuman scream. "Yeow ohh yeow," came from upstream.

"What's that?"

"Don't know. Listen!"

The scream continued in one long breathless wail. "That's Clyde!"

"Come on. Let's find him. Sounds like he's in trouble."

"Ayee ooh yeaw!" The screams didn't stop.

"Ya don't think a bear got him?"

"Naw!" Toby replied as they hurried toward the sound. "You can bet he's somewhere he's not supposed to be, doing something he's not supposed to be doing."

As they went around the bend in the river, they spied the sawmill, closed because the old man who ran it had taken a fall and broke his leg.

An odd sound was mixed in with the painful screams of Clyde as they approached. "Didn't I tell ya? He's messing with the mill. Listen. That's the scream of the saw. It's not just Clyde. Where is he? Ya see him?"

"Nope, not yet."

"There he is, on the floor by the saw. Just squirming in circles. Come on! Hurry! Where's Jake? Oh, there he is hiding in the back corner."

They climbed up the riverbank to the mill floor. What a terrible sight Toby saw. There on the floor was Clyde, holding his hands crossed on his chest, and there was blood everywhere. Clyde was kicking and rolling around in circles. His painful screams were mixed in with the high-pitched screams of the saw. It was an eerier duet they sang.

"Jessie, help me get him down by the water." They each grabbed hold of him as best as they could. As they passed the switch on the saw, Toby reached and turned it off. The noise was instantly more bearable. Toby saw the grizzly sight on the cutting table, and knew immediately what had happened. "Jake, come and help us!"

The boys half-dragged and half-carried Clyde down to the river. They laid him under a willow tree on the riverbank. Toby told Jessie to cut off a hunk of willow bark. In the meantime, Toby grabbed some vines and made a tourniquet. He put one around Clyde's arm above the elbow to stop the flow of blood.

When Jessie appeared with the bark, Toby tore off a piece and shoved it into Clyde's open mouth. Then he forced it shut. "Chew on this and shut up!" Clyde was so surprised that he just obeyed. "Now, Jessie, get a rock and start pounding the rest of that bark. I need some powder."

Toby had jammed Clyde's hand into the mud at the riverside as soon as they had arrived. The sand was red all around. Toby let out on the tourniquet a little to see if the sand got redder. It seemed to stay the same. He eased Clyde's hand out of the mud. There was just a little blood now.

Toby moved quickly. He had little at hand to work with, but what he had he used wisely. He put the hand and arm into the cold water. He looked over the wound. The thumb had been severed through the knuckle joint near the hand, leaving only a piece of skin hanging loose. Toby took the loose skin and draped it over the sawed off joint. Then he took a thin strip of rawhide from his poke and tied it around Clyde's hand while using the skin like a bandage.

"Jessie, do you have some powder for me yet?" He asked as he reached for a broad leaf growing under the tree.

"Some," Jessie replied. "This is hard stuff to grind."

"I just need a little," he said as he put about three pinches on the leaf. "Put the rest in his mouth. Spit that old bark out, Clyde, here's some new to chew."

Toby put the powder on the nub and covered the whole hand with wet leaves. "I need something for a bandage," he said as he looked around. "Let's just use this. It'll do."

"You ain't gonna tear it up none, are ya?" Clyde yelled about his old tattered shirt. "Ma'll kill me!"

"Hey, Jessie, go up there to the mill. See if you can find a can or something to put mud in."

The bleeding seemed to have stopped when Clyde looked at his wrapped up hand. The pain had eased due to all the bark he had chewed. Clyde got a look of panic in his face. "Hey, hey, I want my thumb! I can't go home and leave my thumb!"

Toby yelled up to Jessie, "It's on the saw table. I saw it earlier. Did you find something for mud?"

"Yeah, there's an old paint can. Figure that'll do. Yuck! And here's the cutoff thumb. Do I hafta bring it?"

"Yeah, and come on. We gotta get him some real help. Where'd Jake get off to? There you are. I see you slinking up there in the trees. Come on and help us get him back."

Jessie and Jake arrived with the bucket. Toby filled it loosely with sand. Then he put Clyde's hand down into the mud and filled the bucket to the rim with cold water. The boys took off for home. Sometimes Clyde walked. Sometimes they carried him. The feeling started coming back and the hand throbbed with every step. Jake moaned about as much as Clyde because helping with his brother had turned into more work than Jake was used to doing.

As they passed where they had been fishing, Jessie noticed the traps. "You might know! Just when I was gonna beat you. Look, you've caught two more!"

"Well, I think the fish won today." He stopped and let them all go free. "We'll get them another time."

They worked hard trying to keep Clyde on his feet. He finally fainted. "Out cold! I'll get some water." Clyde responded to the handful of water and tried to struggle to his feet.

"Look!" shouted Toby. "Great Pa's ole mule. I didn't know we had come this far." Toby ran to get the mule for Clyde. As he neared the mule, he looked up the mountainside and saw Great Pa coming down the trail. "Come, Great Pa, we need to use the mule to hurry Clyde for help. He is hurt."

Great Pa loosened the tethered mule and lifted Clyde on its back. He walked beside the mule and helped Clyde and the mud bucket onto the back of the mule. Toby led the mule across the shallow riverbed where he had first tricked the O'Shira cousins.

Having no doctor to go to, Great Pa told Toby to head for the teacher's place. When he wasn't teaching school, Mr. Macon dabbled in animal medicine. He would help.

Great Pa took Clyde in his strong arms and started for the house. "You boys go get his pa. Wait, Toby, you stay and tell Mr. Macon what happened. Jessie, you and Jake head for your uncle's house. Send him on his way here."

So, Toby repeated the story from the first scream to the finding of Great Pa and the mule. The whole time, the teacher was unwrapping and removing a very muddy shirt. When he reached the leaf and the strip of rawhide, he began with the "hmm"s. He asked Toby why he had used that particular leaf. Then he chuckled when Toby replied, "I used it because it was there, and it was wide enough to wrap his hand."

"A very practical reason. It is also a painkiller like the bark. You'll learn that when you study medicine. You are going to be a doctor, I guess."

Toby blurted out, "Oh no! I would rather doctor animals. I like animals better than I like most people." He said this just as soon as Jess and Will, who had been across the road at The Post, entered the cabin.

The uncle glared at Toby. Toby realized that had not been a very polite statement, and he turned red to his shoulders. Will noticed and said, "Hmph, I didn't know Injins could git redder."

Great Pa put his hand on Toby's shoulder and said, "There is much you don't know about this Indian. Come, Toby, let's go home now."

So Great Pa, Toby, and the mule went back across the river toward home. Will watched amazed. The teacher's movements called his attention back to the boy.

"I will dress this with a clean bandage, but I'm not going to remove the skin or the rawhide. If it doesn't all grow back, I can cut off the dead skin later, or you can. Here is a little something to help with the pain. It's going to hurt him for a few days. He'll be alright, but he'll have to learn to write all over again."

The father asked, "Ya mind tellin' me what happened here?"

"Well, I wasn't around for the greater part, but I'm sure Clyde and Jessie will fill you in."

Clyde put his dirty shirt back on. He reached into the muddy bucket with his other hand and slipped something into his pocket as they left.

That day and ever after, if anyone asked what happened to Clyde's thumb, he gave them his own version. He told it so often that he believed it himself, even when Jessie tried to correct him. "Well, I cut it off with the saw. And when I seen what I dun I took off fer home. I's gettin' a mite tared when I seen some ole mule in the woods. Thar I was bar footed, and mite nigh bleedin' to death. So I clum on that ole mule and rid'em crost the river. I cum up on to Teacher's place. I stopped in and he said I's gonna be okay. So I went on home. I don't know whut happen to that ole mule."

To add to his story, he would pull out the thumb to prove it. He had his ma put a string through it and wore it around his neck. It stunk to the heavens until it finally dried out. It was like some old rabbit's foot. It was his trophy until he lost it years later.

CHAPTER 9

That pretty much brought summer vacation to an end. School started with Clyde as the topic of conversation for a few days 'til everyone grew tired of his story. When Clyde told it to some boys one morning, the teacher overheard and looked for Toby's reaction. Toby never even flinched. He went on with his reading and never tried to straighten out Clyde's story.

The two oldest boys had quit school a couple of years ago. There were only three O'Shira cousins left in school. This would be the last year for Jessie. They never went to school past the age of fifteen. Jessie still had a couple of more years. Clyde was the same age of Jessie, but everyone thought he was only about nine. He wasn't as big as the rest of the clan, but he was more ornery.

Jessie had tried to tell the truth, but Clyde was adamant about the whole thing. He reminded Jessie as he spoke quietly into his ear that he better "aught ta remember they wus kin." Jessie came to school the next day with evidence he'd been soundly beaten, and he carried a black eye for weeks. After that, Jessie rarely sought Toby's company alone. He would hang around if others did because he liked Toby, but none in his family did. This went on for most of the school year.

Then one day, on one of those rare occasions, Jessie didn't come to school. Toby wondered about it, but he wouldn't ask Jessie's sisters. School was finally over at 3 o'clock. That still gave Toby time to check his fish traps before dark. He hurried off to the river.

Hmmmm. He knew he had set those traps before school, yet each one had been set out of the water. This had happened a few times before, but never with every single trap.

Suddenly as Toby turned to start for home, there was a soft whisper from behind a pile of rocks. Toby knew there was a little nook in behind the pile of stones. He stopped dead still.

"What'cha gonna do about ya traps, Toby?"

"Oh, hello, Jessie. What are you doing here?"

"I been huntin'." He pointed to a furry pile of rabbits. "I got me a coupla rabbits."

"Good ones. Nice kill. The skins are not damaged."

"I learnt it from you. My skins is the best in the family."

"How come you weren't in school today? I don't ever remember you not being in school before."

"Just practicin'. Pa says I ain't comin' back after the winter break. He says I gotta help out at home. He says I know all I need ta know from any school. I can siphen my numbers and can read fair. He says it's all I need to deal with folks and help feed the family. Since Netty got hitched and moved to town, Ma's been kinda poorly. I think she misses Netty. Anyhow, Pa says he needs help tendin' the family. I think it's cause of Clyde's pa." He ducked his head and looked away when he said this.

"How does that work?"

"Well, Clyde kinda makes out you might a turnt the saw on."

"Now how could I do that when I was with you downstream fishing?"

"I know that, and I tried to tell Pa and Uncle Jess too, but it did no good. Jist got me a heap a trouble. Pa says I ain't ta talk ta ya, er hunt er nuttin' with you anymore. Claims you do black magic er sompun like that!"

Toby stared at Jessie. "I'm the same as I've always been!"

"Well now that's true. But you gotta amitt you're difernt. You've always talked difernt. Now why's that? And you just know stuff. Now why's that?"

"Stuff? Like what?"

"Well, you know. Like, how's you know how to fix Clyde's hand? You can git closer to the animals than anybody I know. And jist disappear in the woods. I see ya, then I don't! You know stuff about yer granpa even when he ain't around fer you ta know. That kinda stuff. I never thunk on it before. 'Til Pa said it. Are you magic? Do ya use some kind of magic Injin stuff?"

This kind of questioning ticked off Toby. He let Jessie have it with both barrels. "I am half Seneca. Indian. The blood comes from a long way back. Great Pa's great pa was the first known to us. We don't know about before him. He was very wise, and had great sight into man's thoughts and the future. He passed parts of these gifts on to his family. I have some of his gifts. Great Pa says there will be more as I grow older. You think I talk different? Well surprise! It's you and your family and these people who some call Hillbillies who talk different. We Seneca are a proud people. We must do things the right way. We speak this way because it's the correct way. Great Pa and my white mother spoke this way to me. They both could read. Great Pa reads all the time. It's ignorance and a desire to be like your pa and your uncle that makes you talk the way you do. There's nothing wrong with family ways – I have them, too. But I don't try to push them on you or accuse you of black magic or something."

"You callin' me a igrunt 'hillbilly'?"

"No, Jessie, you only act ignorant. Your pa is right. You do read well. But, Jessie, think about the stories. Do the people in the stories sound like your family, or even use the words in the same way? Jessie, ignorance is when you don't use the information you have in order to make yourself better with your knowledge. As to calling you a hillbilly, I never have called you or yours any name except the one you told me. I said "some" people call folks here on the mountain Hillbilly. But you know what, everybody here, including you, calls me Injin. And you think it's okay!"

"That's difernt. You are a Injin!"

"Learn to say Indian. It's not so hard for a smart Hillbilly like you!" He started away from the rocks as Jessie stared open-mouthed at him.

Toby paused and turned back, "Oh, yes, about my emptied traps. I'm not gonna do anything about them. If your folks are so hungry that they have to steal to eat, then take them with my blessings. Glad I could help."

CHAPTER 10

Toby had a lot more free time after that. It seems his hunting and fishing didn't take as much work as it used to with Jessie or his cousins always tagging along. In fact, Toby learned to enjoy his solitude once again.

True to his word, Jessie had not returned to school. His little sister, Rose, would speak quietly but secretly to him every day. Clyde became really rowdy in school. He didn't like being the only boy of the family left in school. As a matter of fact, he became so unruly that Mr. Macon sent him home in the middle of the morning one day in November. The note said for Clyde not to come back until he could control his behavior.

It was easy to see how agitated and fretful Rose and her two cousins were. The children continued with their studies, but the girls did so with their eyes darting frequently toward the door. The others understood when the door suddenly banged open with a cold blast of air. They all jumped. They turned as one and saw Clyde's pa and uncle bursting into the room. Mr. Macon very calmly told the class to go on with their work, and they looked back to their books. It was hard to do with all the uproar that had started.

Mr. Macon was no small man. He stood like a big grizzly bear about to protect its young. Toby thought with a grin, "Maybe that's why two brothers came." Toby glanced at little Rose who stood trembling beside her desk. He saw the anguish on her face as she stood in a puddle of water at her feet.

"Please step out, sirs. We'll talk there. You are upsetting my class," Mr. Macon suggested calmly.

"I come to git my girls. Ain't no school what pertects a Injin good enuff fer my kids. Come on, Rose," yelled Jessie's pa.

Toby sprang from his seat at once. "What's he talking about, Mr. Macon?"

"Not now, Toby. Sit down." He turned to Jess and Will. "I don't know what Clyde has told you two, but it's time some truth was spread around this school and this mountain town. Clyde's been going around lying about things ever since Toby fixed his thumb and probably saved his hand, and maybe even his arm. Because Toby stopped the bleeding, he may have even saved Clyde's life. Now what has Clyde said that has happened here?"

Big Jess O'Shira stepped up to Mr. Macon's face. "I ain't blevin' no Injin-lovin' book thumper over my own boy. He said ya whooped 'im fer sassin' that there Injin kid, an' I bleve'em. Blood's thickern water."

"Now that statement is true, Jess. Blood is thicker than water. However, it has nothing to do with this truth. Your Clyde has become a trouble-maker in my class. Ever since Will's boy left school, Clyde has caused an uproar every day. Today was no different. It was a little girl who hit him on the head for pestering her. I should have used the board, but I chose to get rid of the problem instead. Now hear me good, Jess O'Shira, what you do about Clyde is all your problem, but don't let on that Toby or anyone else caused Clyde his trouble here today. Now you keep your thick blood at home. If he comes back to my school, he will respect us all. You get me, Jess?"

"Gotcha, teach. Clyde ain't comin' back. Neither er the rest!"

"Will, I hope you don't let Jess cut off your nose to spite his face. These girls need more schooling."

"I'll think on it, Jim. Fer now, I need'um home. Is it true what'cha said about that Injin kid?"

"Sure is. And his name is Toby Singletree."

"Clyde let on you fixed his hand after he got hisself here. How'd the Injin... err, Toby know how?"

"Well, first of all, he didn't get himself here. Moses, Toby, Jessie, and Jake brought him in on Moses' old mule. As to how Toby knew, the boy reads books. He hangs around here reading my old medical school books. He even takes them home with him. He fixes up the hurt animals in the forest."

"That's hard to swaller, Jim. Anybody else say so I'd call 'em a liar. Well," he turned and eyed Toby while he called to the girls, "come on, girls."

The girls gathered their things, all except for little Rose. Without anyone noticing, she had slipped quietly out of the room during all the loud ruckus.

CHAPTER 11

Toby headed home after Mr. Macon had released the classes early. No one could get their minds back on their work. So Mr. Macon said, "Go on home and try not to let this interruption bother you. Put it out of your minds. Forget about it, if you can."

But the kids didn't forget about it. They went home by the way of The Post, the Smitty's, or any other place they could find a person to talk to about what they had learned that day in school. With the help of the children, the mountain people heard the truth of what had happened with Clyde's hand. Many eyes and mouths popped open with awe and wonder. New respect grew for Toby. Not because of Clyde's thumb, but because he had not tried to feud with Clyde over the lie of the whole matter.

But Toby didn't understand the accusation directed at Mr. Macon by Jessie's pa, Will. He needed to know. He returned to school. However, Mr. Macon was already gone over to the vet's office. Toby went over and knocked on the door.

"Come in." Mr. Macon turned toward the door. "Why, Toby, is there something wrong?"

"No, sir. I just need to talk to you if you have the time."

"Toby, of course I have time. School is over early today, remember? Now, what do you need to talk about?"

"Well, I can't help but wonder what Jessie's pa was talking about when he said you protected Indians."

Mr. Macon couldn't keep from grinning at Toby's precise intonation. He looked at Toby, thoughtfully, for a very long time. So long that Toby finally asked, "Is it something you don't want to talk about? If it is, I can get on without knowing."

"No, Toby, I can talk about it. I just don't know how far back to go. About the time Clyde and Jessie's pa and I were just kids, I guess. We all seemed to arrive here on this mountain about the same time. They were here just long enough to have the whole school terrified of them and their pa, and that included the teacher at that time. But I'm getting ahead of myself. You see, Toby, I was a runaway. I ran from riches and snobbery. I wasn't built that way and couldn't handle the demands my father laid on me. So I decided to make it on my own. That's when I ran smack into your Great Pa. He caught me trying to live off the land. His garden was the land he caught me in. Well he knew I didn't belong on the mountain. So I got the third degree. That wasn't too long after his grandson, your pa, left to go seek his fortune among the "white eyes" as your great-grandfather told me.

Well maybe he was lonely. I really don't know, but he said I could pitch in with him. However, he believed in school, and I'd have to go there. He took me to school the next day and left me. At school and after school, I was whipped soundly by the new O'Shira boys. Then on my way home from school that day, they jumped me again. All three of them were waiting for me after school. The old man over there instigated, and both Will and Jess jumped me at the same time. I took a sound licking that wasn't pretty. When your Great Pa saw me, he didn't ask one question. He just took me over by the fire and started applying his medicine. The next day, I was hardly sore at all, but I sure didn't want to go to school.

Your great-grandfather said something to me that I shall never forget. It changed my life. He said, 'You've already run once. Do you plan on being a rabbit when you are a man?' Well, I went that day and every day after that until I left the mountain.

That day, Great Pa was in The Post when old man O'Shira came in bragging about what had happened, and what lay in store for me that day after school. Needless to say, I had dreaded all day what lay ahead. The day had seemed short to me. When I neared the path to the waterfall, there they were – all three of them. But before we could even spit, there was a stirring in the woods behind us. Great Pa stepped to the path with his bow and arrow loaded and aimed. The whole time, he spoke the arrow was aimed causally at the old man.

'Well now, Mr. O'Shira, I see your boys want to play with my boy. Why don't we just sit over here under the trees and watch. Now you and your boys are new here so I'll tell you our rule. We are fair. So one of you boys come sit over here with us, and we'll let the other one play first'.

Now I was a boy of mountain-size even then. I beat the boys soundly, one at a time. Then suddenly Great Pa roared, 'Oh ha ha ha, oh ho ho. You were right, O'Shira. I believe the boys should all play together'. By the time he let the other boy back in, I had gained my self confidence, and I whipped them both again.

When your great-grandfather finally stood up, he came over to us. Will and Jess were down on all fours panting, and I was hugging a tree. He said, 'Well, Mr. O'Shira, we have chores and I'm sure you do too. It was a pleasure watching with you. Don't you think the boys can play together without you and me now? Jim,' he said to me, as he put his great hand on my shoulder and led me around O'Shira and the boys, 'you should have the boys come and play every day. I believe it's good for you'.

You know, Toby, those guys have shown me respect ever since that day."

"But why did they say I'm under your protection?"

"When you first came here and wanted to go to school, I told your great-grandfather I would look after you. Will and Jess's kids thought I meant I'd whip anyone who messed with you. They didn't realize you were very good at taking care of yourself. But every time you bested them, the boys went home telling that I had something to do with it. Don't be bothered about it. Will and I get along. Sometimes I even think he listens, and maybe heeds what I say. So there is no problem. Does that satisfy your questions?"

"Well, I do have just one more question. It's kinda personal, and none of my Indian business. Great Pa says it will be my white side that will get me into trouble," Toby said with a grin.

"Well, ask your white question." The teacher was enjoying this rare insight into Toby's character.

"How did you get to be the teacher here?"

Jim laughed a big hearty laugh. "Is that it? Well, that's easy. That, too, is because of your great-grandfather. I had only been here a few weeks when he found me at the foot of the falls with my head down and tears streaking my face, and he said to me, 'Well, now what has the great adventurer so down? And you've been off your feed-bag for a day or so'.

'Ah, sir,' I addressed him. I have always called him 'sir' when I address him. It's all I have ever found to be respectful enough. 'Sir, I miss my family an awful lot,' I said. 'Well,' he said, 'why not just go home?' So I replied, 'Three reasons, Sir. They may not want me back. I don't always want to run. And most of all, I don't want to be like them, or to live like them. They are very rich, and they use that fact to their advantage. I don't like that. I love my parents, and I miss them and my sister, but I don't want to be what they are'.

He sat down beside me and said, 'Let's talk about your three reasons. First of all, parents want their children near. I believe the white man's Bible tells about a boy who left home and came back to a big festive welcome home. Now then, don't be afraid of running. There are times when a man needs to get out of the forest so that he can examine the trees. A person who gets away may be able to see clearly enough to go home. A rabbit runs to get away from danger, but he returns when it is safe'.

Then he directed my attention to the great oak tree hanging out of the side of the mountain. 'You see the large tree? It grows from the rock, not from the soil on the ground. Yet it is still a tree. It's different in rooting, but still a tree. The birds have lived in this tree for many years. So does the squirrel. True, the tree is not the same as others, but it does not compel the bird to be a tree, neither does the bird try to be a squirrel. They each are what they were created to be. Man would be wise to learn from the messages nature sends us'.

Well, Toby, two days later I said goodbye to your great-grandfather. I went home, explained the way I felt, and was welcomed home. I went to school. I studied to become a teacher and a vet. Fifteen years later I got a mysterious message saying a teacher was needed here. And here I am!"

"Great Pa being the mysterious message?"

"I'm sure, but I never asked. Now are you content with the answers?"

Toby smiled sheepishly. "I'm content, but I do have a favor to ask."

"Ask. Up to half my kingdom is yours." Mr. Macon swept his arm dramatically.

Toby laughed, "It's not that bad. I was wondering if I could borrow some of your books about herbs and medicines. They interest me."

"Is that all? It would be my pleasure to loan you books. I was wondering where your interests would run. You've read nearly all our books in the classroom."

Mr. Macon chose five books from his wall. "Here, you might begin with these. They even have some Indian lore about herbs and medicine."

So Toby took the books home with him intending to read them as soon as he could.

CHAPTER 12

Just before Thanksgiving, the weather changed drastically. It began to snow about midday. Mr. Macon decided to let the children go home so they would be able to get home without any trouble.

Toby was elated. The air was cold. The snow was wet and clingy. The smell was new and wonderful. It snowed every year here on the mountain, but somehow this one was different. The real difference he would discover a few days later.

Great Pa had asked him to pick up some supplies at The Post on his way home that day. As he entered the store, Mr. Otson called out, "Well hello, Toby Singletree. I suppose you are here for your great-grandfather's winter order. It's a good thing for me that others on the hillside can't get by on so few goods."

"Hello, Mr. Otson. Great Pa said you'd

have a few things that he was out of ready for me today. Guess it'll be extra cause he says this one will be a really hard one."

"That's why he ordered up more supplies. Hope he gets home 'fore it gets too bad out there. He was in earlier today. Said you'd take the stuff home. Where'd he go, anyway, on such a cold day with his big bag of corn?"

"You know he's always out and about. He's probably already home. Thanks for packing this so nice and tight for me."

"No trouble. Here, have a stick of candy to gnaw on."

Toby took the candy and wallowed it around in his mouth as he grinned his appreciation to Mr. Otson.

Toby trudged through a thin coat of snow that became heavier as he climbed. Not once did he cut an animal track. He did, however, smell smoke as he neared the old vacant house. He decided to go nearer and see what or who had a fire going.

It was getting darker, but it was still pretty early. When he came into the clearing, the snow was really coming down hard. He saw a light through the window, a pile of wood by the door, and the smoke billowing out of the chimney. He had thought to see who his neighbor was, but the wind was tugging at his load. He decided he'd better get on home with the winter supplies.

Great Pa was waiting for him out by the truck wagon. The bed of the truck was loaded with bags of corn. The bags were covered with old skins, and the skins were covered with branches from the evergreens that grew all around.

"I scattered corn for miles around. The deer should find enough to get through this spell. Come on in. That load looks heavy. I'll just tuck the ole mule in for warmth."

"Great Pa, there was smoke coming out of the chimney, and a light was in the window of your friend's empty house. I smelled smoke and went over to investigate. The wind was gusting so I nearly lost hold on our supplies, so I didn't go any nearer than the edge of the woods. But I thought you should know."

"Well, I guess Moore didn't like the town after all. He must have come today while I was scattering corn. He will not be prepared for winter. Come, we will go help while we still have a few hours."

As soon as Great Pa and Toby arrived at the Moore house, they went to work. They got the boards from the feed barn and boarded up the windows. Mr. Moore had cut a lot of wood so Toby began to carry it. He

saw how run-down the house was. It had not been lived in for several years. There were some cracks and spaces in the walls. Toby went back home and returned a little later with the wheelbarrow full of empty tow sacks and some nails and a hammer.

Mr. Moore's youngest girl was busy helping her mother and an older sister. She saw what Toby was trying to do, so she went to help him.

"I will help you hang those sacks. My name is Delight. My mother calls me Del. My father calls me Light. My sister calls me Pest. You can call me-"

"Gabby! I will call you Gabby because you talk so much! My name is Toby. Now, if you want to help, work your hands, not your mouth."

Immediately she held up a sack for Toby to nail. They worked silently until the cracks were stuffed, and the windows were covered.

Her mother smiled to herself. That was a long time for Delight to keep her busy mouth shut.

Toby had looked closely at the old fireplace. He kept having strange scenes of fire popping into his thoughts, and he had saved about half a dozen of the sacks.

When he finished, he took the sacks in the

wheelbarrow and went to the barn. "Great Pa, may I use Mr. Moore's shovel? There is something I need to do."

"I'm sure it will be okay. But hurry. We need to leave soon."

Toby took the shovel and the wheelbarrow, and headed for the riverbed nearby. There was a strip of sand beach carved out by the fast moving water. It was wet, but that was good. Here he filled the bags in record time. Then he pushed them back to the house.

As he was unloading the first bag from the wheelbarrow and taking it into the house, Mr. Moore saw him. "Whoa, whoa, what is this?"

"You will need it to put out a fire later, Mr. Moore," said Toby sincerely. He continued to take the bags into the house. He stacked them in a corner near the fireplace.

Great Pa had assured Mr. Moore it couldn't hurt to be ready just in case. "Toby, we should go. It is getting very cold and I have a surprise for you I nearly forgot about."

Toby's eyes lit up with curiosity, but Great Pa held up his hand to stop any questions.

"Thank you two for your help. You, Moses, have always been a good neighbor, and now you too, Toby."

Toby smiled and shook his extended hand. Great Pa said, "Wasn't much, but maybe you will stay warm."

As they walked away, Toby called back, "Stay safe!"

At his words, Mr. Moore wore a puzzled look into the house. "You know, there is something different about that boy. Moses says he knows things that most boys don't, and he's really good with animals."

"He certainly was good with our little Delight."

CHAPTER 13

As soon as they were on their way, Toby tried to ask Great Pa about the surprise. But once again, Great Pa told him to save his breath for the trek home. It was just as well because the wind blew with such force that they struggled to stay afoot. The snow was already growing deep with many drifts. This would probably be one of those winters that the mountain people would talk about for a long time.

Toby ran into the cabin and started a small fire.

Great Pa reached into the truck and drew out a good-sized wiggly bundle. Toby opened the door just as a strong gust of wind sent Great Pa stumbling forward. He fell inside with a pair of panther kittens all over him.

There was immediate pandemonium when the dog became involved. Toby grabbed the dog, and the cats were quickly collared by

Great Pa's enormous hands. When the old dog was controlled and saw no danger to Toby, he returned to his bed in the corner to watch.

Toby watched in wonder as the young cats continued to slap out at Great Pa. Finally, Toby could restrain himself no more.

He reached out for one very carefully. It tried to escape but was soon defeated by Toby's gentle caress. He even began to purr a little.

"Great Pa, where did you find those babies? They must have been late born. Why, they can't be more than four months old at the least."

"You are probably correct. I found their mother caught in a bear trap. She was near death with the bait clamped in her mouth. Hunting must have been poor for a day or two. As soon as I freed her, she leaped away with her prize. She could barely go. I could tell she had newly weaned kittens so I kept my distance so she would go home. It was easy to trail her because she left a trail of blood. She only lived to feed her babies that one last time. I put her carcass in the truck. Her pelt is very pretty. After the kittens fed, I sacked them up in an empty corn bag. They have been quiet until now," laughed Great Pa.

"They will have to stay with us for the winter and I will teach them to hunt so they will survive in the spring," said Toby seriously.

"And now I will call you Mother Panther," replied Great Pa with a raised eyebrow.

Great Pa had covered the windows all but about a foot from the tops. He kept the snow away from the door for a few days, but it was too cold to open it anyway, so he stopped shoveling.

It didn't take but a couple of days for Toby to get to feeling all closed in. The panthers and his old dog were distractions for awhile. He read two or three books and then he couldn't be still.

"This is awful, Great Pa! I feel like I'm choking."

"I've been thinking of moving into the cave. At least we can get fresh air coming around the waterfall."

But Toby was concerned, "What about the kittens, Great Pa?"

"They will stay near you or wherever you put them. It is too cold for them to wander around."

So they moved beds, the tepee, and some new wood. All the activity helped for awhile.

CHAPTER 14

It was cold. Even the cave was cold. Toby had never been so cold in his life. He and Great Pa had built a fire in the cave three days ago. They kept it going all the time. The only time Toby felt warm was when he rolled up in his blanket and lay next to Great Pa on their bed made of animal skins.

"What's happening, Great Pa? I don't remember ever being so cold before."

"Hmm. It has been this cold a few times in my life. When I was growing up the winters were very long. Sometimes we would go north to hunt in the late fall when the animals were getting fat and ready to hibernate. The snows would many times come early. That would delay our return for many days. Now, that was really cold! Living out away from the comforts of the snug tepee.

It was after one of those times that my father built the log house over the opening of this great cave."

"Wow, Great Pa! Do you remember that?"

"Oh, sometimes little thoughts of it pop into my mind.

"Great Pa, tell me about when you were young. You never say. Do you have brothers, sisters, cousins? Tell me." Toby was wide-eyed and curious to know. He never had the opportunity to ask all the things he wanted to know before. Maybe the snow would be valuable yet.

Great Pa only looked very intensely at Toby. He did not smile. He placed his great paw of a hand on Toby's forehead and looked deep into Toby's clear blue eyes. "You know I will not speak of my dead. They are all gone to the greater place. You are all that is left. But you know."

Toby squirmed under the pressure of Great Pa's hand. "Tell me, Toby, what you know."

"This is very strange, Great Pa, but you are right. I know that since Runs Like A Horse, there has only been one male child born to each generation. No sisters. All the wives have been barren otherwise. It was meant to be." Toby began to smile.

"What do you see, Toby?"

"Until me, Great Pa, I see many children playing in the cave. In the field I see strong boys. Three of them. Maybe I am to break the trend, Great Pa."

"Maybe. Be careful. Don't misread your thoughts. Take your time; they will come again."

Great Pa released Toby's head. He turned away to the fire. He got a cup of hot coffee and returned to Great Pa clearly troubled about something. He sat down cross-legged in front of Great Pa. He sipped his hot coffee and looked up into Great Pa's wrinkled but strong face.

Great Pa said nothing. He waited and looked into Toby's sincere eyes.

"Great Pa, I know you have said, 'Do not speak of the dead'. This troubles me much because as you, I get little thoughts in my head. I see my mother and shadows of others around her. She said, 'Don't forget me. Speak of me often'. Now, Great Pa, what am I to do with these thoughts I do not ask for? They really bother me because they come often. I try to push them away but they come anyway."

"Toby, son of all my people, you are very young to be so wise. You are also kind and helpful to others. The old ones on this mountain love you greatly. They see the deeds you do for them in secret and they tell me. You are good for them and for me. The young do not understand you and give you much grief. You will be alone for most of your young life and of course you will have thoughts you do not wish for. But Toby, you are not responsible for your thoughts. You are only responsible for what you do with them. There is an old Indian proverb: 'You can't keep the birds from flying over your head, but you can keep them from building a nest in your hair'. Toby, son, let these thoughts come and look at them, listen to them. Your mother may have guidance for you."

"Thank you, Great Pa. I think you are right. I will think on them. Maybe my head will not hurt so often," Toby laughed.

Great Pa slapped his leg and jumped up. He moved very quickly to a cache in the cave. He returned with a bundle wrapped in cured skin.

"I had forgotten about this. Guess I'm getting old." They both chuckled.

Great Pa opened the bundle very carefully. Inside he found a small wooden box. He handed it to Toby. Toby was about to open it when he noticed the awe and tenderness in the way his great-grandfather rolled open the white hide that was the bundle.

"What is that? I've never seen anything like it before."

"No, Toby, this is very rare. It is also very old. This, Toby, has been the first bed of five generations of Seneca Indians. I see that age is taking its toll on it though. Just look at the scraggy edges."

"But, Great Pa, what is it?"

Toby reached and touched it. In a whisper, he said, "There was a great hunt to get this one. The arrow that killed it belonged to- oops I nearly said his name. He gave the hide to my great-great-grandmother all those years ago and you still have it!"

"Yes, Toby, a foolish thing to do. But each birth made it more important. Since your father was placed on it, each year it becomes more valuable. But as you see, it is crumbling. Falling to pieces. It is worth nothing now to anyone, but maybe me or you. I need to ask you, Toby, to give its total value to me. Do not become attached to it."

"What do you mean?"

"I want you to give it all to me. When I die, I want to be wrapped in this hide and burned as we did your mother. Here. In this cave."

"Of course, Great Pa. It's yours to do with anyway. I'll do what you ask." Toby drew near and took his grandfather's hand, then spoke softly, "Why do you speak of those things to me now? Is something wrong with you? Do you not feel well?"

Great Pa saw that he had startled Toby with his passionate discoveries. "No, no, no, Toby. I was only carried away with strong feelings when I saw the robe. It always does me that way. Just getting old, I guess."

They both laughed with relieved tensions.

CHAPTER 15

My Dear Toby,

Or should I say 'One with the Trees'? I have no idea which name you will choose, but I know it's one of them. You were not to be given this letter until you could read and have some understanding of life. I hope it hasn't been too hard on you. I'm sorry there are no more pictures. The one of our family is all we ever had made. Your father didn't really want this one but I insisted. Do not show it to your great-grandfather. He will not want to see his grandson's image on paper. I know how your father and his family felt about speaking of the dead, but please, Toby, keep my memory in your heart. I am not Indian. I am a Christian. The little testament book I put in this small chest will tell you how to become one when you are older. Look at the picture and try to remember how much fun we had together. Your father made these little wooden carvings for you to play with, and one of ivory for your name.

Grow up to be strong, Toby. Always love your great-grandfather. As long as he lives, never leave him. You are all he has. Love God. Obey Him. Go to the white man's school, Toby. Remember, I always told you that.

This isn't much to leave you, my son. I'm sorry we couldn't be there for you.

Toby, I don't have many more days to be with you. I'm leaving another note in the box for my family. It will tell them who you are. When you are ready, go to them. Go to them. They will help you because you are my son.

I love you hard, Toby.

Mama

There were tears rolling down Toby's face when he finished his mother's letter. He was recalling the game they played. They would hug each other tightly and say, "I love you hard." He hadn't realized he missed his mother so much. He didn't remember his father.

This must be some of the reason Indians didn't talk about their dead. It hurts too much.

Toby replaced the little white buffalo and the bald eagle in the box along with the letters, picture, and small Bible. But he kept the little ivory tree out for himself. It looked like there were tiny arms wrapped around the tree. There was a hole in the top of the tree. Toby would put a leather strip through it and wear it around his neck.

When he closed the box, he took it to his great-grandfather.

"Great Pa, I would like you to keep this box with your robe. I don't think I will need this for awhile anyway. There are some carvings my father made for me and a picture of my family all together. You may look in the box anytime you want to."

"Thank you, Toby, for telling me what is in the box. Yes, I will put it away with the robe, but you will know where it is. I will not need to look in the box." And he never did.

CHAPTER 16

Toby spent the next couple of days reading and working with the cubs. He took raw meat and let them follow the scent. When they did that repeatedly, he began to hide the meat for the kittens to find. They became quite proficient in trailing and finding. He even taught them to spring upon his chest and take away a piece of jerky he had clamped in his mouth between his teeth.

Then one day about two weeks from the beginning of the snow, Toby stopped what he was doing and listened carefully. "Great Pa, I think I hear the river moving with more spirit than usual. I'll go see. Would you keep the dog and kittens from following?"

Great Pa didn't answer. He only tossed out a little meat for each. Not one of the three animals moved from its snack.

Toby worked his way toward the waterfall opening. The water was falling so quickly over the opening that he couldn't see anything through the water. Usually he could see shapes and shadows from inside the cave, but not today. He clapped his hands in joy as he turned around and returned to Great Pa as quickly as he could.

The last few feet, he went running and shouting, "Great Pa, Great Pa, the rivers runs faster and heavier. It must be over. Can we see? Can we see?"

Great Pa smiled. "Calm yourself, Toby. We will open the wall into the cabin. But we might need to stay here for the night, if it is still very cold."

And it was very cold!

They spent that night in the cave with a fire, but they left the cabin wall open. Great Pa even built a small fire in the fireplace of the cabin. The next day, he kept the fire going in the cabin.

"Why do you make a fire in the cabin, Great Pa?"

"The storm is over. People will be moving about. There are no tracks outside as yet and folks might wonder why we had no fire to stay warm. We must keep the cave a secret as long as we can. It is no business of the others."

"I never thought of that."

"Come, let's prepare to go out for awhile and visit the Moores. We'll see how they fared the snow. Gather up some corn and syrup. They may be short."

CHAPTER 17

Toby moved the two kittens back into the cabin. They snuggled in and slept. The old dog lay near the fire and kept a watchful eye on the baby panthers.

It had been a great pastime while in the cave to teach the babies to find their food. He would hide pieces of jerky for them to find. He played a special game with 'Little Miss', which he had named the female. He would put a piece of meat between his teeth and she would grab the other end, and they would play Tug-of-War. Then she would lick his face and nudge under his chin with soft purrs. Toby would scratch behind her ears, and she would run away with her prize: the jerky. 'Sir,' as Toby called the tom, would sit and watch in a bored manner. Sir didn't play much, but he liked to roll around with Toby a little.

Toby was checking on the animals when Great Pa called, "Better grab your poncho; it is still very cold out!"

They both slipped into their blankets with holes cut in them. Great Pa picked up his feed sack with a few food items in it and stopped, suddenly staring at Toby.

Startled, Toby questioned him. "What's wrong, Great Pa?"

A grin started spreading across his face as he answered, "Either your blanket grew shorter or you have grown longer legs since the last snow."

"It is a little shorter today, isn't it? I hadn't noticed before. Wow! Great Pa, I'm nearly to your shoulder."

"Well, come on, let's get out of here before you get too tall for the door."

They left the place laughing and jawing at each other. Toby thought how warm he felt from the love they had for each other. As they traveled to their friends' house, Toby was amazed by how everything looked so different with the heavy covering of snow.

"Great Pa, it is so quiet and beautiful. And so bright. Where are all of the animals? I've never seen it like this before!"

"I guess this is the biggest snow we've had since you have been with me. I thought you of all people would know where the animals are. Especially since your cats in-training wouldn't come out with you today."

"If I would have thought, of course, I know where the animals are! Do you always know things without thinking, Great Pa? You always seem to know before everyone else!"

"Humf!" Great Pa laughed. "No, Toby, I don't know all the answers, but I am thinking all the time. An old 'Injin' like me has to be alert. How do you think I got so old?"

"Funny you call yourself that, 'Injin'. My friend, or used to be friend, and I had a few words back before the snow. He said he thought I was being smart and I said I thought he was being ignorant. Anyway, I guess we aren't friends anymore."

"Well, you never know about people, Toby. Some you can trust for life and others you have to watch and be ready for whatever may come. Take Jessie's family: they have been my lifelong enemies. They are like the coyote. Jessie is probably letting their hate for me rub off on him. You never know about that clan. Just watch and be ever alert."

Toby was about to say more when he saw their neighbor coming down the path toward them.

Great Pa called out, "Well hello, Moore! We were just coming to see how you faired the weather."

"Hello yourself. We just got by, but I'm out to try to beat the coyote to a rabbit or two."

"It is a little soon for the rabbit to poke his head out of hiding, but Toby and I have brought part of a young piglet and some of the potatoes from the spring garden. They need to be used before we lose them."

"What a good neighbor you are! Come back with me, and we will have coffee before you return to your place. Anyway, that girl of mine drives me crazy with questions about you and this here young'un of yours. Maybe he can relieve my ears a little."

"That sounds like a good idea. I think Toby may need a new friend."

But by the time they reached the Moore's cabin, Toby was wishing for a longer blanket to cover his legs because his pants were also too short and the snow was deep on the path. Smoke was swirling from the chimney as they approached. The door swung open before they could get there.

"Git yawls self in outta the cold!" the old woman shouted.

They stomped off the snow from their feet. As soon as they entered, they were led to the fireplace. Everyone scooted aside so the welcome newcomers could take the chill off.

"Hey, what happened here?" Great Pa asked as he saw where part of the mantel and a great deal of the floor was burned black.

"Well, I tell you it's only cause your young Toby there was smart enough to put dirt close by that we even still got a house about us!" Mrs. Moore declared.

"That's durn shure right!" chimed the old man.

"Well, tell us what happened," said Great Pa.

"What happened was about three days into the snow when the wind was all fired strong, it seemed like a backlash happened."

"A backlash?"

"Yes. It sure seemed that way. The kids was all gone to bed so's they'd stay warmer. I's readin' there at the table. Ma'd jist stoked the fire fer the night when a great puff come down from the chimney. It blowed fire right out of the whole fireplace. A big ball of fire caught Ma's skirt tail afire. She set down and started poundin' herself 'n grabbed a rug cover offin the rocker there and throwed it on her. While we's puttin' Ma's fire out, the fireplace plum caught 'n started burnin'. Well I turnt around twice 'n seen them tow sacks of dirt just cryin' out to be used. So I used 'em! They put that fire right out! Smart thinkin', boy! We owe you a lot."

"You don't owe me anything. I just saw there hadn't been a fire in there for a mighty long time. You just never can tell about fires. Anyway, I'm glad everyone is okay."

"Okay! Boy, we're alive thanks to your sand bags. And you're welcome here anytime you want to come by. Ma makes some mighty fine tea cakes."

"Thanks a lot. Great Pa don't make tea cakes!"

They all laughed about that.

"That reminds me. I brought a few things to help tide you over. We probably have a couple more days before we can get down to Otson's."

"That honey you brought before the storm was wonderful," Mrs. Moore said.

"I beat the bears to that last summer. It really is sweet, and there was so much of it. I bet I took five pounds of cone plus a gallon or more honey. I brought you another jar full."

"I'll use some to sweeten a batch of tea cakes. You come on by soon as the weather clears, Toby."

"Thanks, ma'am. Where's Gabby?"

"Who? Oh, she's been sent to do some readin'. School will be starting up again in a week or so, you know."

"Yes, and we'd better be getting on home and get you started to reading, too."

As they plodded back up the mountainside, Great Pa asked Toby, "Why did you suddenly run out the other day to get those bags of sand, Toby?"

"Well, it seemed to me when I turned from plugging the walls I could see sparks and balls of fire jumping all around. I know it wasn't real, but I figured it could actually happen."

"Looks like a good thing you took action on what you thought could really happen."

"Yes, sir."

CHAPTER 18

It had been a very long winter holiday. Due to the early snow and so much of it, the holiday was from Thanksgiving until the end of the year. "No need to go back to school just for a few days," the note on the schoolhouse door read.

It gave the boys extra time for mending their hunting and trapping gear. All the animals were wintering in their lairs, warm and hid away. Many were surviving on the corn and hay that Great Pa threw at intervals during the snow covered days.

Toby spent his time between the cabin and Moore's place.

"Getting to know the Moores," he said. He missed seeing the little smile that appeared on Great Pa's face as he said it.

Toby had missed the close friendship he'd had with Jessie since Jessie had left school. So it felt nice to have someone to pal with. It was a lot different. So far, they only shared their love of books. Gabby loved to read and so did Toby. His reading was more advanced than Gabby's but they enjoyed sitting before the fireplace sharing their stories.

One afternoon, Toby looked over at Gabby and said, "I don't mean to be rude, but can you tell me how your sister got a name like Stormy?"

"Sure I can, and it's not rude! Are you always so polite? It kinda makes me nervous," she laughed.

"Sorry, it's kind of my nature. My mom told me I could catch more bees with honey than with swats. Anyway, it was something like that. And the older folks seem to like it, and I like older folks. So I try harder, I guess."

"Goodness. Sorry I asked. Anyway, to get back to your question about Stormy's name... it's simple. One daarkk and stormy night," she chuckled, "she was born. And that's the way it happened. Ma says she can't remember a worse storm. She says it was thundering and lightning, and the wind was fierce. That ole tree out back of the house was struck by lightning. Ma says it lit up like day, it was burning so bright. And if it hadn't started raining cats and dogs, she said the house mighta caught fire and burned down that very night. Of course it's a good thing it didn't what with the new baby and all. Ma says-"

"Wow. I sure know where I got that name I gave you – you do gab on and on." Toby rolled over laughing and Gabby threw a book at him. Then she joined the laughter because of the surprised look on his face.

Just then Mr. Moore came in with an armful of wood. "Toby, you might oughtta scoot home. It's startin' to cloud over again."

"Yes, sir," replied Toby. "Just let me help you bring in another load of wood." Toby jumped to his feet, grabbed his wrap, and was out loading his arms before Mr. Moore could protest.

As soon as he came back in with his oversized load, he put it in the wood box and said, "Thanks for letting me come read with Gabby. And thanks, Mrs. Moore, for the tea cakes."

"You are very welcome on both counts, Toby. Come again anytime."

Gabby watched him leave from the door. She said, "You like him dontcha, ma?"

"Well, yes," she replied. "He's such a polite boy."

Gabby grinned as she shut the door on the cold.

There was one more good snow. As the

new year dawned, so did the sunshine, which caused the snow to melt in the daytime and freeze over during the night. The kids had a great time slipping and sliding to school that week.

CHAPTER 19

Toby had always liked school and Mr. Macon. They had such a good second semester that spring was on them before they knew it.

The O'Shira boys did not return to school. The girls had come back, but late. Anyway Clyde's sister did. They had been back nearly a month when Jessie's little sister, Rose, returned. She very quietly spoke to Toby every day. No mention was made of Jessie. Her pa didn't come back to visit school again, but Rose came faithfully every day.

One Friday in March, they were let out early. They all ran and hopped and yelled. Toby got his books together and was about to head home in a hurry.

"What's your hurry?" Gabby asked. "Ma said tell you there would be tea cakes if you want some this afternoon."

"Wow, that sounds good, Gabby. Tell

your ma thanks anyway, but I gotta hurry home. Great Pa and I have a pretty important chore to do today."

"What's that? Can I help?"

"No, Gabby, this is something just between me and Great Pa." His great-grandfather had told him not to mention the panther kittens to anyone. Folks might not understand raising panthers since they were hard on people as well as the livestock. As a matter of fact, they were too big to be called kittens anymore. They were nearly grown. That was the chore to be done that day. It was time to turn them loose in the wild.

When Toby got home, he helped bag the cats in large feed sacks. They closed the bags and put them in the truck. Great Pa harnessed the mule to the truck. He laughingly referred to the mule as the "motor." They took the loaded bags several miles from their house.

"Now, Toby, as soon as you find a good place for the meat, you take to the water and wash real good. I don't want these cats thinking it's one of your games. They need to keep going when you turn them loose."

"Yes, sir. See ya in a little while."

The ole mule pulled the truck slowly up the mountain road, but Great Pa didn't mind. He was very patient, and he wanted to give

Toby a good head start. Then, just as the sun was about to drop behind the mountains, Great Pa sat a little taller on the seat and squinted his eyes toward the forest. He thought he saw movement. About that time, Toby stepped out from the trees near the road.

"I thought that might be you."

"Might be me? Weren't you sure, Great Pa?"

"Nope! Sometimes it's hard to find you in the trees."

Toby chuckled, "I found a great place. We need to go on up and across that narrow bridge. There is a place to turn around. Just up to the right of those rocks, there is a small cave near a running stream. I put the meat all around. I left the most in the cave. I bathed in the stream then followed on the rocks back down to the forest until I heard you coming down the road."

As Great Pa turned the vehicle around, he said to Toby, "Now you know you won't be seeing these two critters again. They'll eat up the meat in a day or two, then they will spread out as they hunt. They won't even stay together. They will each find their own territory. They will each be looking for mates in just a little while, and that will take them even farther away."

"Yes, I know. That seems to be the way with nature, huh?"

As he untied each cat, he gave it a scratch behind the ears and sent it on its way. They took to the scent of the scattered meat immediately.

"They act like they haven't eaten all day," Toby exclaimed.

"They haven't," grinned Great Pa.

As they started back down the road, Toby looked back and whispered, "Good luck, Little Miss. Good luck, Sir. Have a long life and lots of kittens."

CHAPTER 20

Toby and Gabby became good friends. She learned how to fish and how to set some of the traps. But Toby would not take her hunting with him.

"Why can't I go hunting with you just once, Toby?"

"Well, Gabby, that is the reason."

"What? What do you mean? 'That is the reason'. You backtrack my own words on me and I can't figure out what you are telling me. Be plain. Tell me why."

"You talk too much."

"That's not true. You… you do so… you're right. You listen."

They had stopped at the edge of the trail to watch some men as they worked. They had watched them for several days as they erected a small building set back a little way into the forest. Today they sat on the side of a small rise and looked down to watch as two of the men put a small sign over the door. The letters read: 'The Church of Christ meets here. Sundays 10:00 A.M.'. They posted another sign on a nearby tree. It said 'Spring Revival last 2 weeks of April'.

"I wonder what that means," said Gabby.

"Come on. We'd better go on home. Chores to do." Toby reached for Gabby's hand to help her up.

"Now see, you talked then."

"We weren't hunting. When we hunt, you chatter like a squirrel."

She glared at him.

"We have to be extra quiet so that we don't alert the animals to our intentions. We also have to walk without snapping and cracking leaves under our feet," he finished just as Gabby tripped and snapped twigs and leaves under foot.

"Guess I'll never be a hunter, huh?"

"Someday when you practice two things."

"Two things?"

"Yep," he grinned. He held up one finger. "Walk quietly." He held up another finger. "And keep your mouth shut!"

She picked up some leaves and twigs, then threw them at him. He ran up the mountainside and vanished into the trees. He disappeared totally in the forest except for his laughter. She stomped her foot at him and turned grinning down the path to her own house.

Great Pa was working near a fire outside the cabin. They had not yet moved back into the tepee because the nights were still cold. Toby couldn't see what he was doing because he had a large blanket around his shoulders.

"Hi, Great Pa! What are you doing?"

Great Pa didn't bother to look around. "I thought I heard the forest laughing. Was it only you, Toby?"

"Yes, Great Pa, it is a good day and place for laughing. It is a lot different to walk and talk in the forest with a girl."

"Do you miss very much your friend Jessie?"

"Yes. But he chose this way. I wonder what he is doing. He should be in school. It is different teaching Gabby about the forest, and I think a lot more to laugh about. Now what are you making, Great Pa?"

"I've noticed that the two of us could use some new hunting boots and some moccasins. So I got out the good deer pelts and am about to cut some out."

"May I help?"

"Of course you can."

"And may I make a set of leggings and a

pair of moccasins for Gabby?"

"Well now. And why, if I may ask, do you want to do this?"

"Today I said some hard things to her. They are true, but hard. She wants to hunt with me. I told her she walks too heavy and she talks too much."

"Hmm. Hard things, but true."

"Well, maybe if she sees I'm willing if she practices, maybe we can work things out."

"Maybe."

"Her feet are about half the size of mine. Will this be enough to make moccasins?" Toby asked as he held up a cutting of deer hide.

"Looks just right," replied Great Pa.

Just across the road on the side of one of the hills that stretched out near Great Pa's cabin sat a sour and very jealous young man. Jessie had been keeping his distance, but he had also been eyeing the friendship that grew between the Moore girl and Toby.

Jessie had tried for weeks to get enough courage to defy his father and go out trapping with his old friend, Toby. Then just as he was about to join Toby one day, he heard a girl's voice. She yakked on and on at Toby and just wouldn't quit. How could he stand it? They, that is Jessie and Toby, always worked quietly together. His sister had told him about the Moore girls return and how Toby had kinda took the littlest one under his wing. Jessie hadn't believed her – didn't figure Toby to be a babysitter. Well, there they were. Just like Rose said. And havin' fun, too.

Jessie was outraged. Toby had thrown him away and took up with a girl. Must be gettin' soft.

Jessie had followed them around for a couple of days and watched from a distance. A far distance. He didn't want Toby to know. "He's not even careful with her around. Bet I could get right up to 'um 'fore he'd notice." But he hadn't tried it. Jessie kept his distance.

Jessie sat and watched as the two across the way worked on the pelts laid out in front of them. He got tired watching and decided to go on back home. His thoughts were eating at him and he wasn't very careful as he scurried up the hill. He snapped twigs as he hurried away.

There was just enough noise for Toby to hear. He looked up and caught a glimpse of Jessie as he was disappearing into the forest.

"Wonder what that Jessie is doing hanging around on that side of the mountain. He doesn't have traps set over there, does he, Great Pa?"

"No, there are no new traps. I haven't seen much of the O'Shira bunch since the snow fell so hard. I did hear the oldest one went down to the town to go into the army."

"Just the same, Great Pa. We need to keep awake. They aren't always up to good."

Great Pa nodded and smiled. Now Toby was taking care of him, too.

CHAPTER 21

At school the next day, there was little time for visiting. Mr. Macon announced the times for the final exams. In a week, each class or level of study would only come to school one day. They could use the whole day to do the exam if it was needed.

Mr. Macon spent time with each level reminding the children of what they had learned and of what they would be held responsible for.

Those not being reviewed could take their books outside and sit under the trees to study. Toby was leaning against the schoolhouse reading a book about plants. Rose took her book and sat about six feet away under a big tree with her back turned to Toby.

"What'd you do to Jessie," she asked without looking at Toby.

He looked up and saw the problem. Jessie was sitting on the porch of The Post across the road. He was watching them. Toby looked back down at his book. "I haven't been close enough to do anything to Jessie since he left school. Why?"

Rose continued to read her book. "He sure is riled about somethin' you done. Come home yesterday maddern' a ole dog what got the hyderfoby."

"No reason to be mad at me. Must be something else."

"Well he's spyin' on you. You better be watchin'."

"Now why would-"

"Toby, come in here, please," called Mr. Macon.

Toby went directly into the school, but he didn't discount what Rose had said.

Mr. Macon was all smiles as Toby walked in. "Well, Toby, are you prepared for this exam?"

"I think so." He returned the smile.

"What I haven't told you is that this is the highest grade exam I can give you here. Not many of my students stick around to take this test."

"Then what will I do?"

"Well, I can continue to study with you. It will be a little different curriculum. I'll borrow books from the town and teach you, or you can go to school in the town. You would pay room and board for the week; then come home for the weekend. The vet there also needs part-time help. There are ways it could be done."

"I don't want to-"

"Wait, wait. Don't make up your mind before you think about it. You've gotta pass everything first. And you need to talk it over at home. You have a lot of options."

"And if I don't pass everything?"

"Well, the way I see it, math could be your only problem. If you fail any part, you'll have to study here another year before you move up. Go on home and talk it over. Pass. Then decide what to do. Now take your seat. I got to get the other children in."

Mr. Macon brought everyone in. He then gave a pep talk. He reminded them they had a week to study and ask questions at school before finals came up the first week in May. Then he turned them out for the weekend.

Toby approached Gabby and asked her to hurry. "I left something hidden for you close to your house this morning. I haven't had a chance to tell you. Let's hurry – I have to get straight home today."

"Oh, Toby, what is it? Tell me or I'll just die."

"I doubt you'll die over it. Just stop gabbing and let's go. We can get there sooner if you don't keep talking."

Much to Toby's surprise, she took off and didn't say a word. He had to hurry to catch up. From the corner of his eye, Toby saw Jessie, hands on hips, down in Rose's face. "Wonder what's going on with Jessie," he thought as he remembered Rose's warning. They rushed all the way to the Moore house.

Mrs. Moore waved at Toby. "Come on in for cookies, Toby."

"Can't, Mrs. Moore. Thanks. Maybe tomorrow. Here. Under this mossy rock," he said to Gabby. "Try these for size."

Gabby sat down on a nearby rock and jerked off her school shoes. "Why, Toby, how nice. These are like yours."

"Great Pa helped me make them."

"But why?"

"So you can learn to hunt. I told you, you have to walk quiet and your mouth shut tight. With these moccasins, you can feel what you're about to step on and avoid snapping twigs. You can practice walking quietly, and I'll see you tomorrow after chores."

"Oh, Toby, thanks o-"

Toby put his finger to his lips and said, "Tight!"

She closed her lips tight, shook her head up and down, then waved as she walked quietly toward her house.

Toby turned to go home and quickly disappeared in the trees, as was his nature. He made a face and soon came up behind Jessie who was desperately trying to find his trail. Toby stopped behind him and very quietly asked, "Did you lose something, Jessie?"

Jessie jumped, startled. "None of your old business."

"Then what are you up to? There are no traps to borrow from up here."

"I ain't stealin' your ole traps either."

"You've been known to do just that."

"Well, I ain't now. I wuz jist passin' by. How'd you know I's here? That ole girl talks sa much I didn't think you could hear nuthin' else."

"Her talking may bother some, but I kinda like it. Why have you been on my trail lately?"

"Not on yur trail. Jist lookin' around." With that, he turned and ran back down his own tracks.

Toby knew Jessie was up to something, but he was in a hurry to get home and talk to Great Pa.

CHAPTER 22

Exams were over and everyone was waiting around for the results. The students had given Mr. Macon a couple of days to grade. Now it was Thursday, and they were all back at school awaiting the posting.

Several men were at The Post, including Great Pa. Mr. Moore came inside. "Well looks like we ain't outgrowed tradition none," he said referring to the gathered waiting group.

"Nope. Everybody still wants to know what's next with school children," one man replied.

Mr. Moore walked over to Great Pa. "Well, looks like my Delight is about to learn to hunt."

"I've heard that girl called Gabby so much, I forget her real name. But you are right. Toby's making all kinds of plans for the next few days."

"They'll only have a few days. We're taking my Stormy down to the flats to live with my sister there. If she passes all her stuff, she can get more schooling if she wants. She's got a job waitin' for her takin' care of some young'uns."

"Sounds good for a girl."

"I'm told Jess O'Shira's oldest went down to join the army," sneered one old man as he spat into the spittoon near the counter.

"Why 'ud he do a durn thing like that? They ain't no war on!"

"Hear he thinks it'll be fun 'n easy money," another fella gossiped.

"He didn't even go past the 5th grade. They won't want him 'lessen a war is on."

"He might cause a war if'n they don't let him join up."

They all got a chuckle out of that.

Otson looked out the window. "Well I see Macon is tackin' up the grades and all the children are runnin' to see what happens next. Guess we'll all know soon!"

As Great Pa and Mr. Moore left The Post to walk home with Delight and Toby, Jess O'Shira bounced upon the porch. Great Pa nodded at him but said nothing. Jess just kept moving toward the store. Mr. Moore didn't even look his way. He grumbled, "I can't stand that man 'er his kin either. The way he treats his wife and family is downright criminal. She's cousin to my missus and I know all about them O'Shiras. Mean. Clean through."

Some of the children had stormed the store and ran in shouting.

"Toby done got the highest marks this school's ever had!"

"Well now, ain't that somethin'."

"He's a good boy."

"He musta cheated!"

"Ain't right. A Injin!"

And the men gossiped on in amazement.

The three children walked over to their parents. After greetings all around, Toby said with a strange look on his face, "Great Pa, I gotta talk to you about something real important."

"It can wait until we get home, Toby. Right now, Mr. Moore has some news that might effect your plans for the next few days."

Mr. Moore chimed in, "That's unless you can hunt in the flats."

"You're not moving back down, are you? Wow, Mr. Moore, we're all just getting to know each other and all!"

"Now, now. Easy boy. We're only goin' for a short visit. Maybe a week, but not longer. Matter of fact, I's gonna ask if ya would kinda look in on the place a coupla times."

"Sure. I'd be glad to, Mr. Moore. When are you leaving?"

"Well, it'll take a couple o' days to git together. Now that Stormy's made her grades, she'll be workin' and schoolin' in the flats."

Toby looked sadly at Great Pa, but he had nothing else to say as they continued on their way up the mountain trail. When they reached the Moore's place, Toby made arrangements to come by in the morning to hunt with Gabby.

They were barely out of sight when Toby started trying to talk seriously with Great Pa.

"Can't this wait til we get home, Toby? I'd like to sit down and look at you for a time as we talk. There is something troubling you and we need some time together. Okay?"

"Sure, Great Pa, it's just that. Well, Mr. Macon said he's-"

"Are you in trouble? Did you fail to make your grades?"

"No, no. It's nothing like that. It's just that I-"

"Well. Speaking of Mr. Macon, that looks like his car parked up at our place. He must have come by the old road."

"Yes, sir. I was trying to tell you he was

coming, but I wanted to talk to you first."

"Well, I guess it'll have to wait a little longer. We have company. Come on, boy. Gather some wood. We'll warm up the pot of stew. We can eat while I hear the news."

Toby had everything going as directed by the time Mr. Macon and Great Pa had gotten past the greetings and the small talk.

They were just sitting down with bowls of chunky meat stew when Mr. Macon asked, "Did Toby tell you I was coming?"

"Well, he tried to tell me, but I kept interrupting him. I didn't get a chance to talk to him. Is there a problem?"

"Lord no, Moses. The only problem is that I knew you would want to know what Toby had accomplished. Also I know he is not a bragger and would probably forget to mention the awards that go with his accomplishments."

"Well, what has he done?"

"He has made the best scores ever made at the school. And he made a perfect score in science."

Great Pa sat his bowl down. He put both hands on his knees and drew himself to a very straight sitting position and looked at Toby for several minutes without saying a word.

Toby's face began to redden as both the

men he loved looked proudly at him. He looked them both straight in the eyes and said, "Thank you both very much for all you have done for me, but I don't want to go."

Then he jumped up and ran into the forest.

"What does he mean, 'go'?"

"He has won a scholarship to a very prestigious prep school in the city."

CHAPTER 23

Toby was sitting outside the church house. This had been his habit ever since he'd taken the job with the vet in the flatland two years ago. He worked all day on Saturdays, spent the night, and fed the animals early Sunday morning before he started home. He would get to the church building just as the singing started. At first, he only stayed for the singing. Then one day he heard the sermon and he became interested. Then he started taking his Bible to work with him, and now he could keep up with what the preacher said.

It was the Bible his mom had left him. He wondered if she had done all the things it seemed to require of him.

He thought he had been unnoticed through the years, but there was one man who noticed and waited hopefully each Lord's day. When they bowed for the last prayer, Toby would disappear into the trees.

Then one Sunday, the man skipped the prayer and walked out in time to catch Toby before he could get away. "Well, hello there, Toby. How is the job going?"

"Oh, hi, Mr. Macon. I was just passing by. It's great, Mr. Macon. Thanks. I really do like it. Gotta go, Mr. Macon. Great Pa needs me. I'll be by this week to return these books."

"Okay, Toby. Maybe one Sunday, you'll come in."

Toby smiled and was gone before anyone else saw him. He remembered how disappointed his teacher had been when Great Pa had agreed with Toby about going away to school.

Great Pa did, however, think Toby should take the Saturday job with the vet. So every Saturday after school started back that year, Toby was up before the sun and blazing a new trail toward the flatlands. For the first six months, he didn't travel alone. Great Pa went with him and taught him some valuable lessons about the land and the forest.

The second Saturday out, Toby had started down the same trail he had taken the first Saturday. "We'll go on a different path today," said Great Pa. "Don't make white man mistakes. Senecas never take the same path two days in a row. Someone may be looking."

"You are right, Great Pa. I learned that playing the game with the O'Shiras when I first came to school here. I knew that. I just wasn't thinking."

"Another white man mistake. Not thinking." He twirked Toby's ear and grinned. "I'll meet you here at your day's end."

"Good journey, Great Pa."

Then one Saturday as they reached the foot of the mountain, Great Pa said, "I'll not be here this afternoon. I think you can get back up the mountain without me. I'm meeting Mr. Macon and we're going to town on business. Good journey," he said as he raised his hand in departure.

After that, Toby came and went to work and home much as a fleet footed deer could move through the forest.

He continued at school with Mr. Macon. Then at the end of the school year, Mr. Macon called him in to talk.

"Toby, I've done all I can for you. You've passed all the subjects I could borrow from the high school. There is nothing more for you here. And you are so young. I want to help send you to college now."

"Don't worry for me or my future, Mr. Macon."

"But Toby," he interrupted, "you need to go on to school, even to college."

Toby held his hand up to stop Mr. Macon. "Sir, I appreciate all you have done for me. And I mean no disrespect. I know you thought I was just a spoiled kid when I wouldn't take the scholarship."

Once again, Mr. Macon tried to say something, but Toby wouldn't let him. "Sir, I must tell you why. I'll never leave this mountain to live anywhere as long as Great Pa lives. I know he would chuckle to think he might need me, but I know that it won't be long before he needs me greatly. So I will not leave. I will live long like Great Pa, so I will have plenty of time to study. I also trust you not to share any part of this conversation with him or others."

"Naturally, I respect your confidence. I'm not sure of your reasoning, but I'll trust your decision."

So, Mr. Macon had arranged for Mr. Moore's girl, Stormy, to take the scholarship. She used it at a girl's finishing school.

Toby went on his way that Sunday and found things very normal. Great Pa was cooking a kettle of stew over the outside fire, but he was not to be seen.

"Great Pa! I'm home. Where are you?"

Just then, Great Pa stepped out of the forest. "Hey, Toby boy, just stepped away for a little seasoning." He dropped some leaves into the stew and they gave each other a big hug. "Well how's it going in the city?"

"The job is great. I love helping the animals that are sick or injured. Doc Johns is great, too. I've read nearly all of his medical books. I haven't even minded staying over on Saturday nights to give the animals their Sunday feed."

"But. It sounds like you have something on your mind. Well, come on. Sit, we'll eat, then we can talk all we want to."

Great Pa went over and sat on a blanket near the fire under his favorite tree. It was a willow that he had brought up from the river many years ago. Toby went into the cabin and brought out two tin pans they liked to eat stew from. He filled their pans and, after giving his great-grandfather one, went over and sat close to the trunk of the willow tree. They ate in silence. Toby helped himself to another plate of stew and turned to ask if Great Pa wanted more. He saw that the old man had put his empty plate on the ground and was nodding off. So Toby ate the rest of his stew and leaned back against the tree. Soon he, too, was taking a Sunday afternoon nap.

Toby opened his eyes with a startle. Great Pa was looking at him with a far away stare. "What's wrong, Great Pa? Did you call me?"

"Not with words, Toby. With my heart."

"What is it, Great Pa? You seem tired."

"I guess I am, Toby Singletree. It takes more of my energy to do things these days. Yesterday I found that old faithful dog dead. When did you see him last?"

"Oh, maybe three days ago. He was acting strange Thursday. He would dart out to the trees then come back where I was working on my bow. When I went to bed, he didn't follow. Friday I didn't see him at all. He usually tries to go with me on Saturdays, but he wasn't on the trail. Did he not come in on Saturday?"

"No. So I went out to find him. I thought he might be in trouble. Sure enough, he'd been into a tussle with a wolf. He had a big enough hunk of the wolf in his mouth to make the wolf run off as soon as he could. The old dog just bled to death, I guess. He had lots of bites and tears in him. He also had a trap mark on his leg. I backtracked him and found where he'd been trapped. Someone had sprung the trap and freed him. Lots of barefoot prints around. I buried him in the cave. Guess that's why I'm so tired."

"I should have been here to do that. He was my dog."

Great Pa chuckled, "That old dog just let you think he was yours. He was the most independent critter I ever saw. He just tried to catch whoever was prowling with the traps and got himself caught. The wolf took advantage."

He spoke barely above a whisper. "Great Pa, there are some things that must be said."

"Speak out, Toby. Never fear or dread to tell me what is on your heart. I will listen."

"Great Pa, I know what I want to be in the future years. I want to be a vet like Dr. Johns. I thought at first I would teach like Mr. Macon. But I would not like that. This mountain will not always be full of ignorant people. The animals will always need care. I have read enough to get me by until I'm ready for school in the white man's world. Please, Great Pa, for now and as long as you are able, I want you to teach me the Seneca ways."

Great Pa put his huge hand on Toby's shoulder and said, "Toby Singletree, you honor me greatly, and I must speak the truth. I may not be able to do as you ask. My eyes do not see as far. My aim is not so true as it once was. My legs are not as strong, nor my hands so steady."

"I know, Great Pa. Even so, I can learn more just listening to you talk than I can running all over to the schools. Please, Great Pa."

Great Pa looked at Toby for a long time. "I feel, Toby, that you have seen something that makes this very important to you. I will do what I can in the time that I have to teach you all that you want to know." Here Great Pa stopped and pointed his finger at Toby. "But you must return to Dr. Johns one more time to tell him face-to-face like a man that you will not be coming back down to work."

Toby dropped his chin down and his face turned very red. He whispered, "Great Pa, I told him two weeks ago that today would be my last day."

"Wha… you are pretty sure of me, aren't you?"

"No, Sir. I just had really high hopes!"

"High, ha ha, hopes. You beat all, Toby."

CHAPTER 24

And so they began. Great Pa took animal pelts from the storage in the cave. He showed Toby how to prepare them and soften them for sewing. Toby was taught to make shirts, leggings, moccasins, and pouches. He even made Seneca artwork on them.

Toby made a very pretty vest from buckskin. He beaded it and fringed it. When Great Pa looked at it, he laughed, "A bit large, don't you think?"

Toby also laughed, "For me, a bit, but I made it for you!"

Great Pa stopped dead still. He picked it up to examine it closer. "Toby, boy, I can't even remember when I was ever given a genuine Seneca-made gift. This is outstanding. Where did you find so many little white shells and beads for the fierce looking white buffalo on the back? It is grand, Toby," he said as he put the buckskin vest tenderly on. "I shall wear this proudly for the rest of my life."

Only Toby knew that would not be for very long.

Toby was shaken. He hurriedly put things away and announced, "Think I'll go get Gabby and trap a little while."

"Good idea. There's some beef jerky I made yesterday. Take some. I won't be here for lunch. I'm going down to The Post to show off my new vest."

Toby laughed as he grabbed his gear and a few pieces of jerky and pushed them into his poke he wore over his shoulder. He went directly for Gabby.

She was hanging clothes out to dry as he approached. "Gabby, you want to go with me to reset traps?"

"Yes, just let me go to the barn and tell Ma and Pa. They seem to need me around more since Stormy is off to school."

Toby sat on a fallen log. He looked around as he waited and listened to the bird. He thought, "Mr. Moore really got things looking good around here."

"Okay, I'm ready to go trapping."

"Then let's get trekking," he chuckled.

They worked several traps. All empty! "That's strange," thought Toby. Then he caught a glimpse of a partial footprint. "Looks like we have help today."

"What do you mean?"

"Well, the traps have been sprung. Not a sign of the catch."

Gabby walked away from the river. AS she walked into the woods a way, she called back, "Look here, Toby. Maybe this explains it."

He hurried over to her. She said, "Look, this one has a rabbit leg still in it and there are big dog tracks."

"That explains this one, but the others are open as if someone opened them. At least this one was stolen by a cat."

"Cat?"

"These are cat tracks, not dog tracks. We had best be careful from now on."

"Toby, cats don't come this close to people, do they?"

"If they are hungry."

"Well, this one ate already!"

They walked quietly on into the forest. At first things seemed normal. Then suddenly, "Do you hear that?"

"What?"

"I'm not sure. I sure wish you'd have worn your moccasins."

"Well, you said, 'trapping', not hunting!"

"I know. It's just that I hear every twig

you snag. Listen, do you hear?"

"I hear nothing, Toby. That's your talent, not mine."

"Shh. That's it! Nothing. No birds. No locusts. The leaves are even still." Then Toby said, "Come on, let's get you home. It feels like we've become the hunted instead of the hunters."

They turned immediately back along the river toward Gabby's house.

"Why are we going this way?"

"To stay in the open. At least we will see it if a cat comes at us. Hurry!"

It was further by the river, but Toby felt safer for Gabby. They rushed on and finally reached a clearing. They scrambled for safety into the barn.

"Oh! Goodness sake!" cried Mrs. Moore. "You scared the daylights outta me. What's wrong?"

"We ran across cat tracks close to home," shouted Gabby.

"Why, Toby, I never knew you to run from anything," said Mr. Moore.

"Sorry, Mr. Moore, I couldn't let Gabby get in trouble. You might keep a sharp eye on your animals for awhile, until we know what that cat is up to. Well, I better get home, too."

"Be careful, Toby, and thanks for the day.

It was fun."

Toby heard Mr. Moore ask if they had found anything in the traps, but he had moved too far away to hear Gabby's description of what had happened.

He wasn't far into the woods before he got an eerie feeling like someone was watching him. He did some backtracking and tricky loops around the trees. He couldn't shake the feeling of eyes on him. He decided he'd better prepare to protect himself if he could. He stuck the leftover jerky into his mouth by one end of it while he searched in his poke for his skinning knife.

Just as he got his fingers on it, but before he could open the knife, he looked up at the shadow in the branch overhead. There, coming at him in full leap, was a huge, black panther. It struck him full in the chest, knocking him down and pinning his hand with the knife under him.

It was a good thing he still had the jerky in his mouth. It might or might not have been the lifesaving item of the moment. Who knows for sure what the cat had in mind. But it jerked the jerky from Toby's mouth and started licking him in the face.

"Little Miss! Oh Little Miss, you gave me the scare of my life. I'm glad to see you."

Toby hugged her gratefully and tugged at her jowls. "You got really big. And what's this? Ahh, you came home to have babies I see. Well, then let's go surprise Great Pa."

CHAPTER 25

At the same time Toby and the panther were on their way home, Great Pa was hurrying home from The Post where he had heard some troubling news about the O'Shiras. They almost ran square into each other.

Toby cried out, "Great Pa, you are traveling just like a white man without watching carefully where you go."

"Ah, Toby, that I am. I have white men on my mind." Then he saw the panther at Toby's side. "Well, look at that! That surely must be Little Miss! What is she doing back here? What are you doing with her? Where are you taking her? Why, she's ready to have kittens! She can't stay here, Toby. Someone will kill her," he finished softly.

"I know all that, Great Pa. What has you so jumpy? Tell me."

Great Pa motioned with his hand. "Come

on. Let's get home and make a warm fire and eat. There is much to talk about."

When they got home, Toby tethered the panther so he could build a fire while Great Pa got out blankets and a big hunk of meat to put on the fire. The cat worried with the tether and tried to get it off, but when she understood it was there to stay, she decided she was too. She walked over and sat down under the willow tree near Toby's blanket and watched as preparations were being made. She cleaned and washed herself as much as a house cat would do. She licked her lips as she enjoyed the cooking aroma.

Great Pa put enough meat over the fire for himself and Toby and laid a big hunk aside for Little Miss. They didn't talk during preparations, but Toby could tell that Great Pa was very upset.

When they sat down to eat, Great Pa only stared at his food, and picked a little bit from the meat on the spit. "What is it that has you so upset, Great Pa?" Toby asked quietly.

Great Pa sat up straight and pointed at the panther who was eating contently under the tree. "First, tell me what you are going to do about Little Miss over there. There are too many people here who would long to take her hide and yours too if you get in the way," he finished with a strange look on his face.

Toby put down his food. He moved closer to Great Pa and cleared his throat strongly before he said, "Well, I had been thinking even before Little Miss came back. There is one more Indian thing I have been wanting to do."

"Oh? And what – please tell me – would that be? I have taught you well all I know to teach you."

"One thing more, Great Pa. I have never gone seeking a vision."

"Hmm."

"So, when Little Miss 'dropped' in on me so to speak…" and here he told Great Pa about the scary adventure with the cat stalking him. He ended it laughing. "If I hadn't had the strip of jerky in my mouth, she might have taken my head!"

Great Pa laughed, "I doubt that. She loves you too much. So what do you have in mind?"

"Well, I need to get away to have my vision, and she needs to get away to have her babies. I was thinking we could travel together up high into the scraggy part of the mountains."

"How long?"

"Oh, I don't know. How long before her

birthing time, do you think?"

Great Pa moved over to the cat. She rolled over on her side and welcomed his large, strong hands. He gave her a good rub down while checking her out. "Soon, Toby, very soon. Maybe two, three days at most."

"Good! If I leave just before dawn, we should have enough time to get her settled in. When she has her babies, she will stay with them. Maybe she will like it up high and will stay away from civilization."

"It sounds like you have thought this out well. I agree with you, but there is something you need to be aware of before you leave." He paused.

Toby waited, knowing he was gathering his thoughts.

"Today I was visiting with old man Otson at The Post. You know how he likes to gossip. He was very excited to tell me that Zeek and Daniel were not away in the army as we had all supposed, but instead they had been in prison over in Alabama. Seems Zeek had a job as a guard for some big automotive factory. When Daniel joined him there, Zeek got Daniel on to work with him. Seems they decided there was more money to be made selling new automobile parts than in guarding and protecting them. Otson said ole Zeek was behaving until Daniel got there. They were pretty slick. It was awhile before they were caught. They got six years, but got time off for good behavior. I can't imagine them being good. They used to give you fits, but somehow you always outsmarted them."

"Well, Great Pa, that is all in the past. I'm sure they are too grown up to bother about me anymore."

"No, Toby, that's the part I haven't told you about yet."

"I thought there must be more."

"While Otson was telling everyone in the store, the whole clan came in. I gathered my purchases and started to leave. Will O'Shira greeted me and mumbled 'Lo Moses'. I returned his greeting with a nod and a 'Will'. This lanky, unkempt young man stood in front of me and looked up at me and said, 'Well, looky here, Zeek, if 'n it ain't that old Injin'. Then Will spoke to the boys and said, 'You young'uns and ya mouths. Ain't no way to tawk ta ole folks'. 'Aw, Pa, he's jist a Injin. Ye don't treat'em like real folks'. Will made a step toward the boy and the boy said, 'Ok, ok. It ain't him I want no way. By the way, how's that breed comin along? I hear he's keepin' company with that lil ole Moore girl'. Then Will stepped in front of me and asked me not to pay attention to the boys cause 'theys jist fresh home'. Well I took my things and left. Your old friend, Jessie, followed me out and said to tell you the boys were looking for trouble. Toby, I'm afraid they may come after you."

Toby sighed and put his hand on Great Pa's arm. "Well, it's like their pa said. They are just baying at the moon. Besides, I'm going to be gone for a few days and I'm sure they will forget all about it after a day or two at home. Don't worry, Great Pa. They are just white men!"

Great Pa chuckled, "I know, but I'm concerned. They looked mean and there are five of them."

"I'm going to tell you something that I know. I've seen me in the future." Great Pa sat up and looked at him. Toby continued, "I thought at first it was you I was seeing, but no, it was me. I will live to be an old man, Great Pa. Right here on this mountain. And there were many children gathered around me."

"Why didn't you tell me before?"

"There was no need. I only tell you now so you will not worry over me."

"And when I die, Toby?"

"I'll be right there with you!"

There was a long silence as they sat and looked each other in the eyes.

The panther stirred and so did Great Pa. "Well now. You have things to prepare."

"Yes, but first I need to go see Gabby."

The lights just went out as Toby stepped into the Moore yard. He didn't hesitate, but went to the door and knocked. "It's Toby, Mr. Moore. I've brought you some deer meat and I would like to speak to Gabby, please. It's important."

When Mr. Moore opened the door, Toby said, "I'm sorry, Mr. Moore. Great Pa and I were visiting and I didn't notice it was late."

"It's okay, Toby. It ain't really late. We 'ums were just tired – that's all. Thanks for the meat. I'll see if-"

"I'm right here, Pa. I heard. I'll just be here on the porch."

"Mind ya do. Not long now, Toby."

"Yes, sir," he replied.

"What's up, Toby? Are you in trouble?"

"Sorta. I have to make an important journey early in the morning. I'll be away for a few days. I-"

"Why? What's going on? How come-"

"Shh. Listen. I have some traps set. I don't want Great Pa checking them alone. If you will help him, I'd appreciate it. You take whatever is caught. I don't want him to mess with any of it, and I don't want you in the forest alone. There is a strangeness going about. Promise me!"

"Well, of course I'll help him, and I promise. Why are you going?"

"Time to come in, Delight," came from the house.

"Coming, Pa."

"I'll explain when I get home. Thank you. I knew I could depend on you. Goodnight." He touched her hand.

"Goodnight, Toby. I'll go over to your place real early."

"No, not before 9:00. He needs rest. I'll tell him to wait for you. Goodnight."

"Night." She went inside.

CHAPTER 26

When Toby arrived back home, the panther was pacing under the tree. Great Pa had a small pack ready for Toby.

"Wow! You have been busy!"

"The cat and I are both anxious. The way she is behaving – I think you need to leave right away. You can be a long way from here by daylight. I'll feel better if she is gone before she is discovered in this area."

"Maybe you are right. We'll leave now. Oh, Great Pa. I told Gabby she can have anything in my traps. They can use a little extra – the pelts, too. I told her she'd be helping you. She's pretty proud. It was the only way I could get her to take them. Great Pa, I don't want her out there alone because the older O'Shiras are on the prowl. They have been known to steal from my traps. I don't want her to run into them. Please wait for her. She has chores to do. Teach her how to take a pelt without making a mess. I haven't had the patience."

He picked up his pack. "There's not much food here."

"What there is, is for Little Miss. A warrior in quest of a vision doesn't eat until after the vision. Then you live off the land."

"I'm not sure I'm up to this. I'm already hungry."

Great Pa chuckled, "You started this. You finish it. Be careful and keep your eyes on that cat. She can help a lot. Which way are you going?"

"Yes, sir. I thought I'd follow the Chattahoochee River down to the Eye."

"Good choice. Stay on the west side of the river. It'll be better for her."

"Okay. Goodnight, Great Pa. I'll see you when I see you. Be sure to wait for Gabby."

Great Pa nodded and waved him off as he lead the panther away from the firelight.

Little Miss seemed to feel the need to get underway in a hurry. She took the lead and moved quickly through the forest. Toby gave her rope some slack and could barely keep up.

Suddenly she crouched down behind a rock and Toby followed suit. They watched as some hunters were moving quietly toward the river. As soon as they had passed, the cat sprang off in the opposite direction. "Where do you think you are going?" He tried to turn her, but she wouldn't turn. She seemed to know something that Toby didn't. She nearly dragged him up into the rocks. She was traveling straight up. Toby didn't know exactly where they were, but Little Miss knew. It was like she was holding the rope and leading Toby.

As the night became paler into day, Toby was growing weary. But they continued to climb. Finally, just as the sun peeped over the mountain, the cat moved behind a huge rock into a small cave. There was a small trickle of water coming down the backside of the cave. She went back and lapped water for a long time.

Toby moved over near her. As he stroked her head and body, he said softly, "Thanks for waiting for water. I hope you can wait two more nights before you have your babies. We are still too close to home. There are men there who would love to have your beautiful fur. They wouldn't care about you or your babies."

She nuzzled his hand then stretched out beside him. Then they both slept.

The sun was high in the sky when Toby opened his eyes. He didn't move for fear of waking the great cat. He looked around moving only his eyes. He grinned broadly when his eyes met the cat's eyes. "Can't put one over on you, huh?" She stretched and started washing herself. Toby looked into the pack that Great Pa had sent with him. He found his hunting knife and a great hunk of meat. When he pulled it out, Little Miss reached out with one big paw and grabbed it.

When she finished eating, Toby watched fascinated as she washed herself. His eyes began to get heavy and he fell asleep in the warm cave.

It was just barely sunset when Toby was awakened by Little Miss washing his face. "Hey! Do you wash everything you see? Okay, girl, let's travel."

Their travel was different now. There was no panicked rush to move her from danger. They traveled side-by-side. She was a good companion. He wondered if she remembered the way they used to play together. Or if she remembered her brother or the old dog. There were no people about and they moved quickly through the night.

The next day and night went about the same. The mountainside was beautiful. They had climbed steadily. There were steep cliffs that looked down on the river. The river itself seemed to have changed. It was wilder with white caps and foam. Toby could see for a long way in any direction. If he could, how much better could Little Miss?

She sat panting at his side.

"Oh, little girl. We need to find you a good, safe place to have your babies." Toby turned slowly, looking for safety for both.

Suddenly out of a crack in the side of the cliff flew a great eagle. Toby stood in awe as the great bird soared high then circled in a spiral looking for food. "He might be a danger to your babies. But look up behind that clump of pines. Let's go see what I think I see." They went higher. Behind the trees, but still in their shadow, stood a big flat rock. And behind the rock were a few others that formed an open-ended cave. "Look, Little Miss! You can have a front door and a back door!"

The panther darted into the cave. She looked around and came back to Toby putting her face in his hand. Toby scratched her head. "Go, girl. I'll wait out here. I have to think awhile."

Toby walked over to the tall pines. He pulled some low branches down and made a tent type from the boughs. He made himself comfortable. Just before sunset, Little Miss came slowly from her cave to see him. Toby gave her a rabbit he had killed on the trail. She took it and walked slowly into her lair. Toby noticed she had started her labor. "Goodnight, girl."

CHAPTER 27

Toby had left the panther two days ago. She was busy and he had things to do. This would be his second night out and still there was no vision. He had not eaten in the four days since he left Great Pa. He had decided this would be the last night out. He was worried about his great-grandfather. "Maybe I'm just not 'Injin' enough," he teased himself. He started thinking back over his time lived on the mountain. He might have been friends with the O'Shiras, but the oldest boys were jealous of him. Clyde and Jake had enjoyed the fact he could best the older boys. They might have been friends except for Clyde's lies when Toby saved Clyde's hand. Jake liked or hated whatever or whomever Clyde hated or liked. It was Jessie he missed the most. He drifted off and dreamed or recalled some of the fun they had as kids.

The eagle soared then dove to the ground

and snared a rabbit by his hind legs. The rabbit squirmed and squealed. The eagle was flying low up the side of the mountain. He just missed the old gnarled, funny-shaped tree. The tree kind of resembled a man with his arms widespread in a welcome gesture. That stance may have startled the eagle. He was so low that he impaled the rabbit against the tree. A stub on the tree caught the rabbit in the center. The eagle did not lose his grip, and he flew away with the lower half of the rabbit. There, on the cross-shaped branch of the tree, the heart pulsated and blood flowed down the old stump.

Suddenly Toby sprang up from his bed atop a flat rock and looked around in a stupor. He came awake slowly. He felt drugged and moved slowly. He recalled that it had been days since he'd eaten.

As he began his trek back down the mountain, he couldn't help but look around for the rabbit of his... his what? A dream? Or vision? The rabbit wasn't there! He approached it slowly. No rabbit. No blood. Just a tree in a dream. Then he heard the scream of an eagle. "Ah, brother eagle, I wish you had some food to share." As he looked up, he ran smack into a berry bush. "Well, brother eagle, in a way you are sharing with me."

He decided to go home and not visit the panther. He wanted her to stay away from his neighborhood, and decided it would be best not to go back to see her. She would be distracted with her kittens for a long time.

He thought he could get home a lot sooner now that he didn't have to hide the panther from people. He had gathered her tether and put it in his pack before he left her. There should be nothing around to lead people to her cave.

A day and a half later, he arrived at his home. Great Pa was not around, so Toby found some smoked deer and ate. Then, because he was tired, he fell asleep under the willow tree.

CHAPTER 28

In the distance, he thought he heard voices. "No, I'm only dreaming."

Then he came awake with a start as someone kicked his foot. "So this is what you do all day while Great Pa and I are out tending your traps," Gabby said with a laugh. Great Pa only chuckled, "Look at your moccasins. You've worn them out. And look at you – you look terrible."

Toby raised up slowly and looked at Great Pa. "Has she been talking the whole time you have been going out?"

Great Pa only grinned as Gabby took another swing at Toby with her foot. Toby jumped up and ran behind the tree with Gabby chasing him.

"Did you eat anything?" Great Pa inquired.

"For the last few days, I've only had berries. I didn't want to use the time to hunt and cook. I did find some deer before I took a rest. Come, let's eat a bite and Gabby can tell me about what she trapped."

She sat down beside him and started right in on the news. "The first day out we had a raccoon and several fish. The fish were really good. Great Pa ate some with us. The pelt is a nice one. It is all spread out to cure. Your great-grandfather promised to help me make a Davy Crockett hat! But Toby, after the first day, all traps were emptied!"

"You mean empty, don't you?"

She looked at Great Pa. "No, the tracks and traps told us, or rather told your great-grandfather, that they had been emptied. Either the animals and fish were stolen or set free."

"What do you think, Great Pa?" Toby asked.

But before Great Pa could reply, Gabby was off again. "That's not all, Toby. Some of our neighbors have been missing stock. We even lost two sheep. And worst of all," tears started to flow, "Juanita Rose that finished with school when Stormy did... she was raped, Toby." Her face turned red because she had said this before Great Pa. She was really upset now.

Great Pa gently helped her to her feet.

"Take her home, Toby. Don't stay. She needs her mother's comfort – not ours."

"Sure, Great Pa." He walked quietly and gently guided her by the arm all the way home. She didn't speak all the way. She cried horribly with great tearing sobs. She was weak when they turned into the yard. Her mother must have heard her sobbing because she was hurrying out the door as they arrived.

"What's going on here?" she demanded.

Toby replied, "I just got home and she was telling me all the news. When she got to Juanita Rose, she became very upset. Great Pa said she needed you – not us. So I brought her home. Can I do anything for her?"

"No, Toby. Your great-grandfather is very wise. I'll look after her now. Thank you for seeing her home."

"Yes, ma'am. I'll check later." And Toby went back up the trail.

Back home, Great Pa was waiting for him. "Is she okay?"

"She cried all the way. I've never seen her this way. It didn't happen to her. Why is she so upset?"

"Girls get pretty emotional at that age. That kind of thing happening to someone she knows didn't help either. She'll be fine. Well, come tell me what happened."

So Toby sat near Great Pa and told him about his and Little Miss's adventure. Great Pa was very interested. "And what of a vision? Did you have one?"

"Nothing to brag about, Great Pa. I guess I'm not a great warrior. I saw nothing to change my name over. In fact, I think I may have only had a strange dream."

"I already knew you would not be a warrior nor would you change your name. You are too gentle and caring to be a warrior, and your name has always suited you."

"So what lies ahead for me, Great Pa?"

"I don't know, Toby. Only God knows for sure. But I think considering all I know about you, if we were still wild Indians, you would be a Shaman. Since we are now tame and live in the white man's world, I think you will be a healer of animals." Great Pa smiled knowingly at Toby. "Now tell me about your strange dream."

So Toby told his dream to Great Pa. He also told him about seeing the tree trunk with limbs that looked like a cross.

Great Pa listened quietly nodding his head up and down. When Toby had finished talking, Great Pa gave a great sigh and sat very still for a long time. He seemed to be deciding something. He made up his mind.

"Toby, I think your vision has to do with your trying to decide whether or not to become a Christian."

"How'd you know I was?"

"May God forgive me for breaking a promise and may my Indian forefathers forgive me, too, for speaking of the dead." Toby was puzzled but said nothing. "Toby, I will speak of your mother. She was very strong-minded. She taught me from the Bible. I came to believe. One day, Mr. Macon and I went to the river and he baptized me."

"But you never said!"

"That is because I promised your mother not to influence you one way or another. That was a bad promise. I should have been helping you understand. You see, Toby, becoming a Christian didn't change my identity as an Indian. It made me a child of God."

"But when?"

"Well, after listening to your mother, I came to believe after some studying on my own. I told her what I was going to do. I went to Mr. Macon's place and he and I went to the river, where he baptized me."

"But I never knew you went to worship."

"I used to go more, but now I find I'm too restless. I've watched you struggle for years as you sat on the side of the hill. I was inside the building. It should have been me who came out to encourage you and not Mr. Macon."

Toby just sat there completely stunned.

Great Pa took a deep breath and put his hand on his chest. "Now let's see if we can figure out your vision. I believe it is about your struggle with the lore of your Indian heritage and the great unknown of becoming a Christian. The eagle is the going off afar of the Indian values. And don't fret over that. Remember we live in a white man's world. The tree cross is representative of Christianity. Now, Toby, you are the rabbit. You are torn between the two. The snagged and bleeding heart may be a warning of all the heartache you may face as you grow up. But you notice in your vision where your heart stays!"

"I don't know what to say."

"Nothing to say. Just forgive me for not speaking sooner."

"Nothing to forgive. I love you, Great Pa."

"And I love you, son of my son's son. Now I'm all used up. I need to go rest."

Great Pa got up slowly and went into the cabin to bed.

Toby built up the fire and studied his

mother's Bible long into the night.

CHAPTER 29

The next morning, Toby stuck his head inside the cabin and saw Great Pa just standing there. "How do you feel, Great Pa? Okay?"

"Oh yes, Toby. I'm just not as strong as I once was in the early morning."

Toby smiled and asked, "Do you think you are strong enough to walk up to the waterfall pond and baptize the son of your son's son?"

Great Pa started doing an Indian dance and war whoops. "You have made my day. I feel strong enough to take on a bear." He rushed to Toby and hugged him.

"Well I hope the bears have enough sense to stay in the country today," he laughed. "Give me about an hour. I want to check on Gabby and go invite Mr. Macon. You want me to come back here or meet you there?"

"Come back here. We'll go there

together."

"Okay. See you in a little while."

Toby stopped by the Moore's place. They were all out doing chores. Mr. Moore waved from the barn. Mrs. Moore was hanging out the wash and Gabby was bringing the fresh milk to the house. As she approached, Toby asked, "How are you today?"

She replied, "I'm sorry I was such a baby yesterday. I'm trying to do better from now on."

"No need to be sorry. We're friends. We should be able to share. Bad and good. And that's why I'm here. In about an hour we are going to the waterfall pond so that Great Pa can baptize me. Wanna be a witness?"

"Oh, Toby, how wonderful! Can I bring the folks?"

"Yes, you may," he grinned.

"Ohhh, you."

"See ya there. I'm going to get Mr. Macon." And off he went running down the trail. It was the same trail he had misled the O'Shiras down the first day of his school. Was he 5 or 6? He didn't remember. He had lots of fun teasing them. He had not realized he'd caused them to hate him so much.

He heard loud talking and laughter. Speaking or thinking of the O'Shiras, there they were just ahead of him. Toby quickly faded into the trees. They didn't see him, but he could see them. They were headed for the river with their fishing gear. "Wow!" Toby was surprised at the change in them. Zeek and Daniel looked as old as their Pas. Jake and Jessie were nearly as tall, but not as old looking. Clyde still looked like the runt of all of them. The whole bunch looked like they had just spent the last week sleeping in their clothes. Jessie was the only one with combed hair. It looked like he might have had a haircut this month. "I can't believe we used to play together," thought Toby. He worked his way around to the back of the school where he found Mr. Macon in his little clinic. He looked up as Toby entered.

"Well, you are out early. To what do I owe this unexpected pleasure?"

"Good morning, Mr. Macon. I've come to invite you to a baptism if you're not too busy."

"Well hallelujah, Toby. I'm never too busy for that. When and where?"

"We're going to waterfall pond. I'm going back for Great Pa now."

"Well, I'll just close up now and come with you. Your great-grandfather must be overjoyed!"

"You should have seen him. He was acting like an Indian doing a war dance or a rain dance or something," laughed Toby.

They spoke of many things on their way to get Great Pa and go to the pond.

Toby inserted, "Hey, I came onto the trail of some of your ex-students this morning."

"Oh yeah, who?"

"All five of the O'Shira cousins. I guess they were going fishing. Anyway, they had their fishing gear. Good looking gear, too."

"Hmm. I didn't know they even owned anything but sticks, string, and cork!"

"Maybe the big boys came back with some army back pay," jested Toby.

"Umm hmm. There's your great-grandfather now." He waved to them. "You know it may take awhile for him to wash off that smile."

"Looks good on him. I hope he keeps it the rest of his life!"

"Well, where's Gabby? I expected her to talk us down by the time we arrived at the pond. And how are you, good friend?" he asked Mr. Macon.

"Well and happy," he replied.

"I suppose he told you all about this."

"No," replied Mr. Macon. "He only invited me to a baptism. I assumed it would be his. I'm pleased. We've watched him struggle a long time."

"I'm afraid a lot of that has been my fault, but it's good now. Where are you, Toby? This deer will be overdone by the time we get back."

At that, Toby stepped out of the cabin. He was dressed in moccasins, leggings, and the shirt Great Pa had made for him. He said proudly, "I want God to know who I think I am, and I want Him to have all of me, my father, and my mother."

"Let's go," Great Pa said with a catch in his throat.

Mr. Macon couldn't speak.

Leave it to Gabby. As soon as she saw them, she broke the silence. "Oh, Toby. How nice you look. You put on your Sunday best and it's only Saturday. How exciting this is!"

"Well let's step into the water," Great Pa said after he greeted the Moores.

The waterfall was roaring. They had to stand close to hear each other.

"Because of the noise, we should hear Toby's confession here."

"Okay," Toby said. "I confess that I believe that Jesus is the Son of God."

"And now, Tobias One With The Trees Singletree, I will take you to deeper water and submerse you in the name of the Father, the Son, and the Holy Spirit for the remission of your sins."

With that said, he took Toby's hand and led him into the water hip high. No one could hear his words, but they could tell he was speaking as he put Toby under, and was crying after he brought him back up.

As they started back, everyone was clapping their hands and Gabby ran out to meet them. Toby swooped her up and carried her back. Both of them were soaked.

Great Pa laughed, "Sorry, Toby, I only brought one blanket. I didn't know Miss Delight would be taking a swim!" He threw the blanket around her shoulders.

"My, aren't you formal today," she said, and snuggled into the blanket.

Great Pa said, "Now if we can gather close, I will ask Mr. Macon to lead us in praise and thanksgiving for the event. Then everyone is invited to our place for a feast – Indian style!"

After the prayer, they all hiked back to Great Pa's place. They sang hymns, laughed, and talked noisily all the way.

They attracted the attention of the O'Shiras, who were prowling up and down the river. They watched at first, and then decided to go closer.

One of them said, "Watch out, that Toby has got eyes in the back of his head, and ears like a-"

"Don't worry. That gal's got him so busy, he can't see nor hear!"

They snickered. "Don't chance it. If'n he so much as looks our way – git! Quick as ye can," whispered Jessie. He don't never let down. I watched him too many times not ta know."

Toby and Gabby were sitting under the willow not far from the others, but apart from them.

As usual, Gabby was talking. "This is great food. I didn't know you could cook corn underground like that. Your great-grandfather knows lots of neat things."

"He's lived a long time."

"I like him a lot. Maybe he will teach me to-"

"Gabby, er, Delight, I have something to say to you," stuttered Toby.

She looked startled. "What is it? What have I done now?"

"Two great things have happened to me today. You witnessed one, and caused the other."

She frowned. "What did I cause?"

He smiled. "We've been friends for a long time. We have kinda grown up together. I never knew until today what you really mean to me. When you came running to me into the water, it was all I could do to keep from kissing you right then and there!" He began to turn red in the face as she stared open-mouthed at him. He continued, "I want to ask your father if I can come calling on you."

"But, Toby, you already call on me!"

"No, Delight, I want to come courting you with marriage in mind, if you will."

Now her face was turning red. "Oh, Toby, you silly. Of course I would love it for you to ask my Pa."

Toby started to get up. She said hurriedly, "Not now, Toby. Come to my house."

He smiled and started to sit back down when he heard a limb fall from a distant tree with a "wumph."

He looked around. He called out, "Anybody hurt?" But all he got for an answer was a lot of scurrying noise.

Mr. Macon joined him as he looked around a little. "Must have been a family of bears trekking past and something startled them."

"Yeah," Toby replied, "a whole family." He and Great Pa exchanged knowing glances.

"Well it has been a great day, and I need to get back to the clinic. So I guess I will see you two in the morning!" said Mr. Macon.

"Wait, we'll walk back part way with you. We need to go, too. Moses, it has been a good day. Thank you so much for letting us be apart of it."

"You're always welcome. Come some more."

Mrs. Moore put her hand on his arm and thanked him as Gabby kissed his cheek and looked at him and Toby.

"See you in the morning on the inside of the building, and not through the window!" They all laughed as they left.

Great Pa asked, "Now what about our drop in guests, could you tell me?"

"There was a knee print and a hand print near the tree limb. There were several different prints scattered in several directions. Guess they changed their minds about a visit."

"All the same, be sharp, Toby. Be sharp."

In the meantime, the O'Shiras had finally stopped dodging trees in their efforts to get away and not be detected by Toby or the others. They all sat at the river panting. Zeek said to Clyde, "Why're you all wet?"

"Well," Clyde said still gasping, "I had me

a good speed, 'n I let up on I's on the water 'fore I knew it. I jist couldn't stop an' I run clean into the river!"

"Clyde, you's always dumber'n dirt," Jake chimed.

"Never mind. Did you hear anything perched out on that limb like a ninny?"

"Nope, I'as too busy trying just not to fall off. Then I heard the limb crack, and down I went."

"Well, did anyone hear what was going on out there today? What was the gathering about?"

They all shook their head no and just looked at each other.

"Well then. Fer now we carefully keep his traps emptied and watch," said Daniel.

Jake said, "He shore seems taken by that purty lil gal."

"Just cool it, Jake. Watch'n wait."

CHAPTER 30

Sunday morning Great Pa had spoken to the preacher when they entered the little building. There was no great stir when others arrived and noticed Toby with his great-grandfather. They had all expected it to happen one day. They sang, they prayed, they took the communion, and the preacher preached. When he finished, he asked everyone to sit for a moment. "Moses has something on his mind to share."

Great Pa stood and bowed his head for a second. "Brothers, I committed some sins worthy of prayer. Please ask God to forgive me for breaking a promise I made to Toby's mother; also I broke a taboo long held by my people. I spoke of my dead. I hope this doesn't ruin your trust in me. And now to the most important announcement. Please stand, Toby. Family, meet a new babe in Christ. Just born yesterday!"

All twenty members broke out in cheers and applause. The preacher led in a prayer for both of them. Then he said, "It will be nice to have you inside the building from now on." He asked Moses to dismiss them much to Toby's pleasure.

As they stood around outside after worship, they heard someone tearing down the mountain in an awful rush. Everyone turned to see Bob Harvey tearing toward them as fast as he could. As soon as he reached them, he blurted out, "My Faye Beth has done been grabbed. Help me find 'er, please."

The preacher took his arm. "Where'd it happen? When? Slowly now. Tell us."

"We pickin' berries up on the west a the river. We'uns, her ma and me, we hear 'er yell an' went to see. She up an' gone. Jist gone. Her bucket and berries scattered all over, but she's gone. Jist gone. Help me find 'er, please."

Mr. Macon said, "Toby's the best tracker we've got."

Toby asked, "Were there tracks?"

Bob looked at him puzzled. "I don't know. I was lookin' fer her not her tracks."

"I'll go with you, Mr. Harvey. But please, Mr. Macon, keep everyone here for a little while so the tracks won't be messed up with helper's tracks. Give us a twenty-minute head start. You ready, Mr. Harvey?"

"You bet. Let's hurry. She may need us."

It took about half an hour to reach the berry patch. "Now, where's Ma?" Bob said frantically as he looked around.

"There behind the berry bushes. She's praying, Mr. Harvey. Go to her and please stay there so I can look around."

"Right. There's 'er bucket," he pointed.

Toby walked carefully around, then went to the bucket. He couldn't tell if she had dropped it or pitched it away from her. He couldn't find anything – no tracks. No sign of a struggle. "Where was she the last time you saw her?"

"Well, let's see now. I don't rightly know. Do you 'member, Ma?"

"Yes, she started at that fer end on the other side an' was gonna work her way to meet me on the side."

Toby walked around and looked again. There at the very end of the brush was a place in the dirt that looked maybe like someone had shuffled the dirt around. Toby was puzzled. Not one footprint other than Mr. and Mrs. Harvey's. Not even Faye Beth's. "There's not one footprint. Not even your daughter's," he said.

Ma fell back to her knees and shouted, "Oh, Lord, ye done took my girl."

"Now, now, Ma," Bob tried to comfort her.

"I'm going on up the way," Toby started moving in a wide arc up the mountain. Then he heard a soft moan. He stopped dead still and listened as he looked. He heard it again. He moved again. Suddenly he saw signs of a person being dragged. But there were no signs of who was doing the dragging. Soon he saw Faye Beth propped against a tree rubbing her head. Her clothes were torn to pieces. "Oh no!" he called over his shoulder to Mr. and Mrs. Harvey. "Here she is, sir. She needs her ma."

About the same time, some folks from church arrived and Toby ran down to meet them. "She might need your doctoring help, Mr. Macon. You better go on up. She's been attacked pretty badly. Probably you folks should go on home. She's been found and she may not want to face you folks. Mrs. Harvey might need a little help from a couple of you ladies."

Folks started moving about. Toby went to Great Pa. "Strange thing. There are no tracks. She was carried then she was dragged the best

I can tell. And Great Pa, I think she's been raped."

"What about the dragger's tracks?"

"That's just it. There are none!"

Then the Harveys were coming down the mountain. Bob was carrying Faye Beth and someone had put his suit coat over her. Mr. Macon was following close behind. "I'll have a doctor come see her if you want me to," he said. "I've done all I can."

"Don't bother. We kind take ker of our own selves," was Bob's reply. "Thanks to all youins fur helpin' out."

"What is that all over her face and hair?" Toby asked Mr. Macon.

"Are you ready for this? It's animal feces – several kinds of animals. Not fresh, but bad enough. She has a huge gash on the back of her head, and she's been raped."

About that time, Gabby came over to where Toby was standing. She had a stricken look on her face. "Don't come by the house for a few days. I'm not up to company."

"Sure," he said. "I understand. I have some traps to mend and some catching up to do with Great Pa."

Everyone went on their way home. Toby took Great Pa's arm and guided him to everything he had found. The scuffled spot near the bush with none of Faye Beth's tracks leading away, but of everyone else's tracks leading away. "She had to have been carried, and she's a pretty hefty girl. Now, here, suddenly she was dropped and dragged. But only her drag marks are here. It has to be someone pretty strong and pretty smart to do this."

"I don't know anyone that strong on this mountain, and certainly not anyone that smart. Has to be an outsider," retorted Great Pa.

CHAPTER 31

After three days of coming home empty-handed, Toby was getting pretty agitated. His traps were always empty and about half of them were needing to be mended.

He told Great Pa that he was going to Otson's Trading Post and then he would come back by Gabby's house.

Toby had made his purchase and turned to leave when into The Post came the three youngest O'Shira men.

Jessie muttered a greeting of sorts and Toby replied, "Well hello, Jessie. I see you still have your shadows. Where are your leaders? Gone to re-enlist? I hear there may be another war about to start."

"Well," Clyde smarted off not wanting to be outdone, "we hear you've been losing yer catch out'n yer traps!"

Toby answered with a smirk. "Hmm. That's strange. I don't remember mentioning that to anyone."

"Maybe we heard that from that little Delight what's always foller'n you around," Jake said, trying to cover for Clyde's error.

Toby walked on past the boys shaking his head and saying, "Strange, very strange." That was for their benefit, but he knew.

Toby went over to the school. The children had been let out for lunch. He walked back to Mr. Macon's office. He stuck his head in the office door. "Hey, are you busy?"

"Never too busy for you, Toby. What's on your mind?"

"Oh, nothing really," he answered as he looked around the floor at the new boxes stacked there. "I was just over at The Post getting some things to mend my traps. They've been slightly abused lately, and the animals don't seem to stay caught."

"Seems there's a lot of that going on," Mr. Macon said.

"Well, Clyde just told me who was doing it. That is, mine anyway."

"Really? And who is that?"

"Oh, he didn't know he did. It's what he said that told me. What is all this? Are you moving?"

Mr. Macon chuckled, "No, no. I'm like

you. I'll never leave this mountain. I love it here. Everything and everyone is real. No, those are the overflow from Dr. Johns' office. It's ether and medications. He does this every so often. If he gets more than he can store, he sends his overflow here for me to store or use as necessary."

"He taught me how to use ether. It's a pretty good medicine."

"Yes, it is. It keeps the animals still while I help them."

"Well, I need to push on. I saw you were out to lunch and thought I'd say hello."

"Glad you did, Toby. How's Moses?"

"Mr. Macon, he is really slowing down. He doesn't do much anymore. Everything tires him out, but he is still cheerful. He must be nearing a hundred. He has never said. We don't mention birthdays."

"We were talking about wars one time and he mentioned that he was a boy of about fifteen or sixteen when the Civil War came to the river for a little while. But it was too wild for them to use so they moved on down to the south."

"Well, I'm off to see Gabby and check my fish traps. Come see us!"

"I may just drop by this week some time."

"Good. Great Pa likes your company."

Toby was off with a wave. He took the trail that was well worn from The Post to the Moore's place. It had probably been forged over the years. He thought as he moved into the forest, "Time is strange. I never thought of age before. Some of these trees were only saplings when Great Pa hunted and surely played in this forest. Why, that means that one day, you little sprigs will be grandfather giants when I am the Great Pa of the woods. So if Great Pa is about one hundred, and I'm, what, about nineteen, then he must have been around eighty when I was born and going on sixty when my pop was born. I just never thought about that. He's been like the trees: always there." He said aloud, "Huh!"

"Huh, what?" said Gabby as she stepped around a fat tree.

"Oh! I didn't see you there."

"I guess you didn't. You were in some other world. What you got in the package?"

"I'm going to repair some traps that have been damaged," he replied.

"I want to come, too. Just let me tell Pa where I am." She ran off to the barn calling her pa. He stuck his head out the barn door.

"Pa, I'm going to the fish traps with Toby."

He waved at Toby and called, "You kids

be careful now."

"We will, sir," Toby called back.

"By the way, Gabby, have you spoken to the O'Shiras lately? Any of them?"

"No, I haven't seen them in ages. Why?"

"Well, I just saw them and they were hinting that they may have spoken to you."

"Are you jealous?"

"You know it!" He grinned at her. "Well look at that. That's one trap we won't have to pull. There's a lot of tracks around. Those guys don't care if I know who is stealing my fish."

They sat on the ground and removed some of the net for the traps. They worked silently for a long time. Then suddenly Gabby started speaking softly, "Faye Beth said she kinda felt a presence behind her, but before she could look around, someone grabbed her arm. That's when she cried out. Then she was clobbered on the head and went black. When she came to, she had a sack of nasty stuff over her head. Her clothes were being jerked off in pieces. She could hear grunts. Said it sounded like their old pig when he was rootin' around in the mud on a hot day. Then she said someone grabbed her again and she fainted. It's a mercy she don't remember no more. God's own mercy. I'd just die if that happened to me."

"Aw, Gabby, I know it's not good and it would make you feel bad, but surely you'd not want to die over it. That's a bit harsh."

"Oh, Toby, I'd be so ashamed. I'd just die. And both Juanita Rose and Faye Beth are very different now. They are very quiet and withdrawn."

"Aw, they'll get over it. Come now, let's go back. I want to talk to your Pa about us."

"Not yet, Toby."

"Why not? You act like you don't want me to speak to him. Have you changed your mind?"

"No, it's just, well, everything will change."

"Now how will it change except that your Pa and Ma will know how I feel?"

"But that's just it. We won't have these freedoms. You'll have to come to my house formally. I won't be able to go out trapping and fishing with you."

"Why not? We're still the same people."

"Yes, but now they'd say it wouldn't be fittin'. We'd be watched all the time. I'll have to behave more lady-like!"

Toby laughed and reached to help Gabby up. "Come on, you. I can live with those changes. Besides, it might be fun to see you act more 'lady-like'."

"All right then. But first, I want something from you."

"What would that be?"

"Leave your stuff here and come with me to the woods. We won't go far. Now keep in mind, I only want one."

"Gotcha!"

They hurried into the woods, Gabby practically dragging Toby.

"Okay, here we are."

Toby looked around puzzled.

"Toby, you've never been anything but a friend and a gentlemen toward me. Now before my Pa puts his 'my daughter is being courted' face on, I want you to take me in your arms and kiss me like you like me a lot."

Toby's heart began to race. "That's technically two thing, but I can manage to wrap them into one." Toby reached for her and she stepped into his arms. The trees held their breath as Toby tenderly and sweetly covered her mouth in their first kiss.

When he could speak again, he said, "Miss Delight, I'd better hurry to your house and speak to your Pa for my own protection."

This time Toby did the dragging.

They rushed to the water, put the trap out, gathered the stuff, and walked hurriedly back to Gabby's house.

Mr. Moore saw them coming, nearly running down the trail. They were laughing so he knew they were okay. "What's goin' on here? A bear after you or another cat?"

"No, sir, I'm just bringing Gabby home so I can speak to you for my own protection," he laughed.

Gabby swatted his arm as she went on into the house.

"Now, what's this about?" he asked.

"Well, sir." Toby gulped. "I'd like your permission to come courting Miss Delight."

"Well now, I like your manner," Mr. Moore said grinning. My Delight is only sixteen. Just what do you have in mind? Marriage?"

"Oh, no, sir." Toby blushed. "We are both too young for that. Besides, I have nothing to offer. I'd just like to be able to tell the world she's my girl!"

"Well, then. Why don't you and Moses come for supper tonight and we'll talk about all this?"

"Yes, sir. What time about?"

"Come about dark."

"We will, and thank you, sir!"

Toby flew up the mountain with long strides to tell Great Pa. Those were the last happy moments to come.

CHAPTER 32

When Toby reached home, he found Great Pa wrapped in a blanket and sitting near the fire. He motioned Toby near. "Run down and get Mr. Macon for me. Okay?"

"Sure, Great Pa. Are you not feeling well?"

"Just need to talk to him tonight."

"The Moore's asked us to supper tonight."

"Go by and tell them we won't be able to come. Tell them we'll be gone for a few days."

Great Pa lifted his hand to stop any discussions. "I'll explain later. Just hurry back. I have things I need you to do."

"Sure. I'm off."

He went first to Mr. Macon to be sure he caught him.

"Well, hello again," Mr. Macon greeted him.

"Hello. I'm here with a special request.

Great Pa wants to talk to you right away."

"What's it about, Toby?"

"Don't know. He said we'd be gone a few days. That's all I know."

"I'll go right away."

"Good. I have another message to deliver. See you later."

Toby hurried on to the Moore's place. He was concerned about his great-grandfather and wanted to get back home. When he reached the Moore's, the Mr. was out in the yard. "Hey, Mr. Moore," Toby called.

"Well, boy you must be hungry. Ma ain't even started supper yet," he grinned.

"Good. That's what I'm here about. Great Pa said we can't come tonight. He says we are going on a journey and we'll be gone a few days. Will you tell Delight for me? I gotta move on – Great Pa might need me."

"Yep. I'll go in an' tell Ma not to do no extra for supper. Moses told me he'd probably be makin' a trip soon. I'll just come by directly and say my goodbyes. See ya later."

Toby went straight home. Great Pa was waiting for him. "Toby, boy, I hate to spring this on you sudden-like."

"What, Great Pa? What's wrong?"

"It's time for me to go to the Great Hunting Grounds. I should go alone, but I want you to sit with me. I don't want to be alone."

"I will, Great Pa. How can I help you?"

"I need you to build me a cot in the cave near the entrance to the waterfall. I'll show you how when I'm ready. Cut some green limbs the size of your arm. Pack some food from the cabin, and Toby, get some blankets ready to go."

"Yes, sir." Toby was very calm on the outside, but there was turmoil on the inside. He had just about finished his chores when he looked up and saw Great Pa's two friends coming up the trails. "They're here," he said.

"Good. Tell Moore to come on in by the fire, and keep Mr. Macon company for awhile. It won't take long to tell Moore goodbye. I already have unofficially."

So Toby met the two men. "Mr. Macon, Great Pa asked if you would wait while he speaks to Mr. Moore for a few minutes."

"Sure I will," he said as Mr. Moore went on to see Great Pa.

They were silent as they watched the short conversations between the long time neighbors and friends. They saw Mr. Moore lend a hand to raise Great Pa to his feet, and watched as the two men hugged each other. Toby turned away.

"See you later, Toby," Mr. Moore said as he passed on his way home. Tears were falling down his cheeks.

Toby took Mr. Macon's arm and they approached Great Pa as he settled back in his blanket. The men shook hands and Great Pa motioned for Toby to be seated with them.

"How can I help you, Moses?"

"My friend, the time has come for me to take that journey I have told you about. Toby will come with me to help me on my way. In a few days, he will return alone. You are prepared to answer any questions that may be asked?"

"Yes, I am. It will all be legal. I must take your vital signs."

"Do what you need to then explain what we've been doing over the past year."

"So Toby," Mr. Macon began, "we started when you were first working for Dr. Johns. Your great-grandfather and I drove to Macon Co., and my father, who is the best lawyer in the state, drew up an airtight will. No one can break it. And all during that time, your great-grandfather, with my help, has been purchasing more acres. You two own a lot of this mountain. There is money in the bank for you when you need it. Your great-grandfather has been a wise investor since you moved here. Call on me, Toby, when you need me." He looked at Great Pa. "You need to make a move. He hasn't much time. I will date his certificate two days hence. Don't show up here before then. Read me?"

"Yes, sir." Toby was pale. He rose and walked away. Once more leaving two old friends to say goodbye.

As soon as Mr. Macon left, Toby ran away, put the fire out, and scattered the ashes. He helped Great Pa into the cave where he had put all that they required. He started a new and cozier fire. He went back outside to make sure they were gone and had left no sign. He closed the cabin door and joined Great Pa.

Great Pa spoke softly, "You have been a bright star in my life. You and I have been closer than I ever was with my son or grandson. You gave me lots more years. A reason to live, you might say."

"I love you, Great Pa. You have been my mother, my father, my great-grandfather, my teacher, and most of all, my best friend." Tears were falling down his face.

"Here now, Indian warriors don't cry. Remember I told you that years ago."

"You remember I told you I'm only half an Indian warrior, and it is the half that isn't

Indian that is crying."

They both laughed at that.

"Toby, the most awful thing to face is loneliness. I read somewhere, 'The brave can stand firm when danger threatens. The strong can endure the treatment of pain. The valiant can stand the darkness of fear; but none can combat the despair of loneliness'. Someone named Lesley wrote that. I never knew if Lesley was a man or a woman. I do know loneliness can ruin a life. Don't be lonely, Toby. Marry that little talkative girl. She won't let you be lonely."

Toby moved over to sit near Great Pa. "Your old buffalo skin smells bad. How do you stand that?"

"Guess I've lost my sense of smell!" he grinned. He directed Toby in the making of his trellis. "Don't mourn too long, Toby. And I give you leave to speak of me after I'm gone. Just don't call my name. That's the real tradition. I know it's hard to part and stay behind. I've done it with all of my family except you. But for me, this is the easiest part of life. No more of what life offers. I go to God."

With that, he walked slowly over to the trellis. Toby helped him get up. Then he spread the white buffalo blanket over Great

Pa's body. "Rest now, Great Pa. I'll see you in the morning."

"Could be. Maybe so, maybe no. Love you."

"I love you."

Toby heard no sound from Great Pa for the rest of the night, but he didn't close his eyes once. He prayed and thought of the many things that Great Pa had taught him and said to him.

Toby didn't know what had changed, but suddenly he was very lonely. He walked over quietly to check Great Pa.

Great Pa reached for Toby's hand. He smiled tenderly and squeezed his hand. Great Pa died. Toby wept. He pulled the buffalo hide over Great Pa's face. With the knife Great Pa had given him, he cut off a small piece of the hide and took it to the nook in the cave where he kept his private things. Then he set the wood on fire beneath the trellis.

CHAPTER 33

At the end of two days, there was no trace of a burial. Only ashes remained from the fire. Toby put a small tin of ashes in the cove with the other mementos he kept. He walked out through the waterfall observing the lay of things. It was dusky dark. No one was around. He walked out on the shore and whistled for the mule. It wasn't long before he joined Toby at the pond. They swam across together. They climbed high on the other side where they spent two days journeying from home and were gone for two more days before starting back. It seemed like an eternity to Toby. They came back by the same way and went straight home. When they arrived, the mule went off into the forest and Toby took out some jerky. He ate as he looked all around. He saw an old horse drawn truck. He chuckled. That should go in a museum.

He heard someone coming up the path. It

was Mr. Moore. "Oh, Toby, I'm so glad you are finally here."

"What's wrong, Mr. Moore?"

"It's Delight! Come, I'll tell you as we go to my place. Your great-grandfather is with his people?"

"Yes, yes. What about Delight? Tell me."

"It was about three days after I was at your place. Delight said she would go check your mended fish trap. I said wait and I will go with you. She said she would only go to the one near the house in the river. I said okay, but come straight back. She didn't and I was mad and went to look for her. She weren't there! I called. She didn't answer. It was like that Faye girl. Only her prints at the fish. Then they wasn't anymore. I ran up an' down the shore callin' her. Then finally I found her in the trees. It's awful, Toby."

"Is she hurt bad?"

"The only hurt we can find is the cut on the back of her head. She 'as raped, Toby!"

Toby fell to his knees. "Oh no, God! Help her through this. Please keep her strong."

"That don't seem to be the worst part. She could get over that. Anyways t' other girls did."

"What do you mean? What else is wrong?"

"Well, Toby, she jist sets there. In a dead stare. She don't talk ner move ner nothin'. We're hoping you can help. Maybe she'll talk to you."

Ma came running out of the house to meet them. "Oh Pa, that doctor wants to put her in a hospital so's she can be fed and watched an' stuff."

"We aint' got no money fer that! Ma, we jist ain't."

"May I see her?" pleaded Toby.

"Go on in, Toby. The Doc's in there, too."

Toby went in quietly. He looked at her and remembered her words, "I'd just die, Toby." He shuddered. She was sitting there rocking herself to and fro.

He squatted there in front of her and whispered, "Gabby, it's Toby. Fight back, Gabby. I'll help you."

She stopped rocking. She looked directly at Toby. Tears were flowing down both their faces. She whimpered then started holding herself and rocking again. Toby stood up and faced the doctor. "Doc, can you help her?"

"I think so, son. But I need her in the hospital."

"Please, Mr. and Mrs. Moore, let her go with the doctor. I know where to get the money."

"We don't take charity, Toby," said Mr. Moore.

"This isn't charity. I love her. I need her. Put aside your pride, sir, and think of Delight. Please."

Mrs. Moore stuck out her chin and glared at Mr. Moore, but she spoke to the doctor. "Take her to your hospital, doctor."

Mr. Moore's shoulders drooped. "You are right, Ma, as usual. Toby, take her to his automobile."

The doctor headed out to make a place in his car for her. Ma grabbed a clean apron. "I'll go be with her, Pa."

Pa agreed. Toby swooped her up in his arms and took her out.

He watched them leave then he left telling Mr. Moore he'd see him later.

Toby went directly to see Mr. Macon. Mr. Macon gave the children an extra recess when he saw Toby enter the school. He rose and met Toby at the door. "I'm so sorry, Toby. You've had a double barrel shot at you. How can I help?"

"I'm okay. My great-grandfather left me his strength. It's Delight that I need to help. Mr. Macon, money was mentioned at Great Pa's place the night you came. Is there enough to pay Delight's hospital care? She has gone there today. If there's not enough, tell them I'll work for them or anything."

"Whoa, whoa. Slow down, man. Let me assure you there is enough and more. When you have the time, we need to discuss your holdings. Are things finished with your great-grandfather?"

"Yes. He has joined his family. He was sent in the style he chose and in the place he chose. I did exactly as he asked," Toby reported. "Now, Mr. Macon, do you know what happened with Gabby? I couldn't get much from Mr. Moore. He was too distraught to know what to tell. Just tell me all you can, please. I intend to find this man."

And the teacher knew if anyone could, it would be Toby. "Toby, it was like the other girls. No tracks, hit from behind on the head, and animal feces in her hair and on her face. No tracks, Toby. How can that be with all that transpired?"

"I don't know. But there has to be something. I'll be looking as long as I have sunlight. If you will take care of the hospital, I will go to the forest."

Toby went home and changed into his leggings and moccasins. He took his hunting knife and an empty pouch. He wore no shirt.

Great Pa would think the Seneca had returned to the mountain.

Toby didn't know where Juanita Rose had been attacked so he decided to look at the other two places for some kind of track. He went to the river first. He checked his fish trap and found it messed up again. He looked very carefully for, what? He just wanted to find something. He made small circles and large circles, but nothing else. He did this until he came to the tree line. Then he sat down in the trees. He listened. "Where is my insight when I need it?" He began to get a sensation that someone was watching him. He raised his head and moved only his eyes very slowly from left to right. Nothing. He moved his eyes back right and left. Still nothing. Not a sound, not a movement. Even the insects were hushed. Now why would the insects be silent except that they had been disturbed? Toby stretched and rose to his feet. Then suddenly the forest sounds were back. Strange.

The sun had headed west and was leaving shadows in the Blue Ridge Mountains. Toby decided he'd go back to Mr. Macon's office to see what he had found out. The man was not home. His car was gone, so Toby decided to wait. He moved across the road and planted himself next to a large tree. He dozed of to sleep.

He awoke with a start. Voices. Where was he? Oh, yes. The voices were those of the O'Shiras. Toby sat and watched as five grown "children" moved toward The Post. They goofed. They managed to hit, wrestle, or slap on the back everyone who came near them. They continued to loud talk while they sat around with the others and bragged and drank their sodas.

Suddenly, Toby remembered the dream he was having before the voices woke him. He had dreamed a little boy warrior with long braids down his back and a bow and arrow in his hand was running from five redheaded little snow-white boys who were chasing him with fish in their hands. He nearly laughed at the memory.

Just then, he saw a car light coming up the road. He decided to wait until the lights were off to step out of the trees.

When Mr. Macon got out of the car, Toby walked over to him. "Hey, Toby. Have you eaten yet?"

"I had some jerky this afternoon. But I'm hungry. You invitin'?"

"Sure thing. Come on in. I made stew before I left."

"Were you able to see Gabby?"

"No. But I talked to the doctor. She was sleeping and being nourished with tubes in her arm. He thinks she'll come around in three or four days. And I made arrangements to pay the bill."

"Good. I owe you a lot."

"No, I still owe your great-grandfather a lot. Here, try this. You must be starved."

"This is great. I can't remember the last meal I had. It's been jerky for several days."

Mr. Macon joined Toby with his bowl of stew. "Now, did you find anything? Do you know any more than you did?"

"I can't understand. The only traces are leftovers from those helping."

"I'm sorry, Toby. You'll find him. I know it." He pushed back his bowl. "Are you ready to do some talking?"

"Sure, what's on your mind?" Toby asked.

Mr. Macon looked at him a minute. "Do you know how rich are you in worldly goods?"

"How can that be? Great Pa and I only had each other."

"When your great-grandfather was younger, he found gold somewhere. He never said where. He began buying land and deeds from people in trouble. You know why so many folks on this mountain had such great respect for your great-grandfather? Of course, other than the fact that he earned every bit of it."

"No, sir. I always figured it was his age."

"Maybe, Toby. But he, and now you, own the majority of this mountain."

Toby just stared open-mouthed.

"Of course, he never made anyone move. That's why the older folks make their young'uns use good manners around Moses. We put in the contracts that when the Mr. and Mrs. of the family he dealt with died, the next generation would have to move on. Now land isn't all you have. There are lots of stocks, bonds, and cash. And, Toby, you don't have to wait for a will to be probated. He put everything in your name the day you turned eighteen. I am the trustee until the day you want to change things. Oh yes, he left a small token will. It's to be posted on the announcement board over at The Post. It simply says: 'Everything that I own or might own, I leave to my grandson, Toby Singletree. He can do what he wants with it'. Of course, everything has been legally yours for about one and half years now. I need you to sign these papers. I have thirty days to make this public at The Post."

Toby signed the papers. "Can you give me two weeks? I don't want people looking at me differently or treating me differently. I need to think on all this before I decide anything about my future."

"Of course you do. You can do what you want. You are legally protected. You can look over your holdings anytime."

"Then I'll go start thinking. Oh, is The Post mine?"

"Yes."

"Does old man Otson know it?"

"Yes."

"Then can I go tell him I want him to do something for me and he probably will?"

"Yes."

"Well, goodnight then and thanks for everything."

"Night, Toby."

Toby went across the road to The Post. Things were quiet now and Mr. Otson was preparing to close. "Evenin', Toby. I hear your great-grandfather has passed on. Sorry to hear it."

"Thank you, Mr. Otson. Did he owe you anything?"

"Nope, we're even."

"Good. I'd like you to do business the same way he did, except when you want to collect or pay, please see Mr. Macon. He will take care of my business for me. Oh, yes. Did the O'Shiras ever pay you tonight?"

"No, Toby, they never do."

"Put their charges on their father's bill respectfully from now on, please."

"And when they all complain – fathers and sons?"

"Tell them it's the policy of the new owner. They'll soon understand."

"Yes, sir," he replied happily.

"Goodnight." Toby left The Post smiling.

CHAPTER 34

Finally the day came when Toby got word that he could see Gabby. Mr. Macon had told him at worship that morning.

She was almost her normal self, and they were getting ready to leave when Toby arrived.

"Hello, Gabby. May I come in?"

"Well of course. I understand we owe you a lot. You paid for all of this."

Toby winked. "You owe me nothing. The money was Great Pa's."

"I might a knowed," said her Pa.

"I see you are preparing to leave. I don't want to be in the way. May I come by to see you this evening so we can talk?" Toby inquired.

Gabby wouldn't look at him as she continued to gather her things. "No, Toby. I'm not going back home. Stormy is out making arrangements for me to go to her home over in Clayton. I don't want to live here anymore. Not on this mountain."

"You'll change your mind," said Toby stepping nearer. She froze. He whispered, "What about us?"

She said, "There is no more us. Now or ever. I'm too ashamed."

"But, Gabby-"

"No, Toby, go away please. Go live your life."

"But you are my life," he pleaded.

Mr. Moore came to lead him out the door. Toby made no fuss. He said, "Mr. Macon will know where to find me when you change your mind. I love you, Delight." He turned to leave.

"Toby." She walked near him and whispered, "There was more than one."

He started to ask something and she shook her head in a panic. No one else knew this. So he turned and left the room. Toby watched from behind a great tree as she got into the hired car to be taken to her sister's house.

When the Moores came out, Toby approached. "Is she going to be okay, Mr. Moore?"

"That doctor says she will. I'm sure gonna miss her."

"You aren't going with her?"

"No, me an' Ma will have to stay here. 'Sides, I just can't abide cities. This one is bad enough. How you gettin' back home?"

"I'll just walk. I've done it lots of times while working for Doc Johns. Come visit and tell me the news." He turned toward the mountain and home.

Toby went home in a daze. He was still stunned at Gabby's attitude.

When he reached home, he felt even worse. Great Pa had gone and now Gabby. He made a fire and rolled up in a blanket. He had a hard time going to sleep. Then he started dreaming again. The five little white boys continued chasing the Indian boy beside the river. Soon the people and places changed. The little Indian became a man with Toby's face. Then the really white boys became the five O'Shira men. In his dream they had eyes of fire and they chased him, getting closer and closer. Toby's feet grew heavier and heavier. He couldn't seem to move and they were getting closer. They were no longer near the river. They were in the forest. Suddenly he knew this was the place where Juanita Rose had been ravaged. They were nearer and nearer to him. He awoke in a cold sweat.

"Whew! That was scary," he said to

himself. "That seemed awfully real." He tried going back to sleep, but he kept seeing the scene in his dream. "I know that place. I wonder if that is the place. I'll go in the morning."

At first light, Toby was ready to go. He covered the fire pit and was on his way.

This was the place. Toby had been here many times during his search the last few days. As good as he was at tracking both human and animal, there was just no trace. Why? There had been three crimes of passion committed on this mountain, one right here. There should be some clue, some clue. He looked up in the trees. Marks from a rope were visible on the tree. "I'll climb up there later." He searched the ground beneath the tree. There were only trampled ground and a few broken pieces of brush-leavings from the neighbors who had found the crumpled girl.

Toby crawled around in the nearby brush. There was nothing but a little ball of sheep's wool. Strange, sheep hadn't grazed here in over a year.

Suddenly Toby realized something was wrong. His head came up as he listened. Nothing. No birds chirped. No squirrels chattered. The forest was dead still. Even the insects held their breath.

The blow came from behind. He sank into a sea of blackness. He had been hit in the head with a tree trunk.

Toby felt as though he was trying to swim to surface from a very deep black sea. There! A tiny gleam of light appeared. It was a long way from him. His memory rushed in on him. He was about to yell out when he suddenly realized his debilitating position.

Toby's arms were back over what felt like a fence post. His hands were tied with rawhide against his stomach. There was another post or branch or something under his knees, and his ankles were tied to the branch that was under his arms. His legs were spread apart in a squatting position and a wedge was fitted from one knee to the other. It was impossible to move. As his head cleared more, he found that he was on his face hard against the ground.

He moaned in protest and instantly a burlap sack was jerked down onto his head. Had he remained quiet one more minute, he might have discovered the identity of his assailants. "That's what Gabby meant. There are more than one."

He caught a glimpse of a small fire and what appeared to be several small sheep running around.

Toby didn't have time to sort this information. He began to gasp and fight for air again. The sack he'd been blinded with smelled strongly of animal urine and feces. It had been used to carry home alive some of the trapped animals.

He felt himself being lifted from the ground. Next thing he knew, he was swinging upside down. With a jolt, he knew he had no clothes on. He could hear the laughs and obscene grunts.

He yelled and screamed at his abductors, but the sack muffled his words. The more he struggled, the greater the frenzy around him became. Only when they began touching his body did he know what they were going to do. They spun him from one to the other with his buttocks in the air and spread apart because of the way he was tied. He felt them rub against him as they worked up their frenzy. He began feeling their firmness against him as their intentions became clear. He held his breath hoping they were only playing rough.

Then he felt someone grab the post at his knees and pull him upward. At the first violation, Toby went wild. "I'll kill you! I'll track you down and kill you!" He said no more because of the filth that got into his mouth when he tried to talk. He had never felt so helpless in his life. All he could do was flounce around in space, and that just made things worse.

One after the other – each in his own time – raped Toby. He was covered in semen, spittle, and tobacco juice from his attackers. Someone, in his excitement, had even urinated on him. They thought it was funny so they all decided that was a good insult.

Just as they were spent from their passions, Toby was exhausted from his anger and helpless struggle.

Toby could tell by the sounds that they were resting. Deep breathing, heavy sighs, and no moving about. Time dragged by, though it seemed like hours. Toby made no sound for fear of calling attention to himself again. He just swung there in silent circles. First one way, and then the other.

Suddenly Toby knew he was alone. They had moved away without a sound, just leaving him hanging. Now he understood Gabby. He was hanging from a tree, naked, ashamed, and full of hate.

They had always been very careful not to leave a trace, not a clue. But this time they had chosen the wrong victim. One of them had made a mistake. He should never have laid a hand on Toby's body. Toby knew that hand. It had no thumb!

CHAPTER 35

The day after Mr. Moore arrived home, he decided to go see Toby. It was a long walk from Doc Johns' place and Toby had not been in the best shape when they had parted yesterday.

When he arrived at the cabin, all was quiet. The fire was scattered and cold. Deep concern settled on Moore's shoulders. He looked around some. Finding no trace of Toby, he decided to go see the teacher. He would know what to do.

Mr. Macon had just sent the children home for the day and was walking up toward Toby's place when he saw Mr. Moore coming down the trail.

"Have you seen Toby today?" they both asked at the same time.

Again at the same time, "No, I haven't."

Mr. Moore grinned and frowned at the same time. "Well, I'm a mite worried. He was purty upset when I talked to him last."

"Let's go to his place."

"I just came from there. Ain't nobody there. It's quiet 'n deserted like."

"Well," Mr. Macon said slowly, "He did say a few days ago he would continue to look for signs until he found something. Maybe he has returned to the rape scenes. Let's go look for him."

The two men searched until they were exhausted. They decided to sit and rest before going to the last place they could think of to look. As they sat near a stream in the shade of the trees, they were startled by a strange muffled cry.

"Listen!"

"That's just over the bank."

The cries became more persistent as they neared the top of the stream bank.

"Wha… who'it," stuttered Mr. Moore.

"It's Toby! Help me cut him down."

They scurried around trying to help. They couldn't untie the knots, so they both took out their knives.

Mr. Macon finally relieved Toby of the smelly, nasty, animal-used tow sack. He was spitting and clawing at his face to rid it of the animal feces that clung to his hair and eyes and nose. Immediately upon the release of his hands and legs, Toby grabbed his clothes that had been tossed carelessly aside and started toward the stream. He stumbled and fell several times because of the numbness from being tied for such a long time.

Mr. Macon found the rest of the attire that Toby had worn and the two men walked quietly to the stream where Toby had headed.

As they approached, they observed him sitting in the water scrubbing himself raw with mud. He rubbed and rubbed. "I'll never be clean again."

"What happened?" Mr. Moore whispered.

Toby looked up at Mr. Moore with huge tears in his eyes, running down his face, and in his quivery voice, he said, "Oh, I'm so ashamed. I was so trite when this happened to Gabby. I'm so sorry. I was flippant. I thought it was no big deal. I'm so sorry. I just didn't understand. Oh my poor Gabby. Mr. Moore, would you tell her it'll be taken care of for both of us if it's the last thing I do in my life!"

Mr. Moore nodded in the affirmative and turned away.

Mr. Macon said, "This brute has got to be stopped. Do you have any clue as to who he is?"

Toby looked deep into Mr. Macon's eyes. He didn't say a word, but the teacher knew that Toby knew who did it. "Can you prove it, Toby? The laws will take care of it."

"No, sir. I can't prove anything, but I know and I'll take care of it myself."

Toby's answer sent shivers down Macon's spine. "Now, Toby, don't do anything crazy. Don't do anything to mess up the rest of your life."

"My life is already messed up. Would you two friends do something for me?" Both men turned full attention on Toby. "Please, sirs, don't tell anyone how you found me or what happened to me!"

"You should know without asking that we would never mention any of this to anyone. And, Toby, I know you will feel strange even around us, but you never need to feel shame. We both care about you."

Mr. Moore nodded his agreement even though he was too moved to speak.

"Now if you both will understand, I need to be alone for awhile. I need to get myself together."

So Mr. Macon put all of Toby's things in a neat pile by the edge of the water. The two men looked long into the eyes of the other with full understanding that each would never mention today to anyone else. They both went their separate ways to their homes.

Toby continued his mud bath. When he finally gave up on his bath, he just sat in the stream praying to God and saying repeatedly, "Gabby, Gabby, dear Gabby. Forgive me!"

HE FELT LIKE KILLING. He wanted to kill each of them, one at a time. The feeling shook his emotions even more. He dressed. He went back to the limb he'd been tied to. He gathered the rope, the sack, and the piece of wool caught beneath some brush. He went home to the cave.

He took out his box of little parts of his life. He felt the piece of white buffalo and some of the things Great Pa had given him. He handled the toys his father had made. Then he read and reread the letter from his mother.

Toby's stomach growled. He smiled and rubbed it remembering it had been three days since he had anything except jerky to eat. He was too overcome with his emotions to care. He slept.

Toby began to dream. They were all children playing in the forest. They hid, ran, climbed, and chased each other. Suddenly all the boys were chasing him. He ran in a panic as an eagle pursued him also. The boys changed into vicious men trying to hit him with tree branches. The huge eagle swooped down and wrapped his talons into Toby's shirt, then lifted him above the heads of his tormentors. His weight was too much for the eagle. The eagle lost height and soon slammed Toby's face forward into a cross-shaped tree. There! Once again, the cry of the eagle as it shrieked off into the blue. Toby was startled awake as the shriek of his dream became reality. Toby sat very still as he thought of the vengeful dream he had just awakened from. All that he had learned from the other Christians and what he had read in his Bible just did not make sense with his vision. The vision seemed from the Indian running in his blood. The vision left him with a strangely strong urge to give in to his native feelings.

Toby began to walk slowly toward the waterfall to exit the cave. As he stepped through the water, an eagle dipped low into the brush growing from the wall across the river. The eagle carried a struggling rabbit in its talons. The eagle, in its haste to avoid the brush, impaled the struggling rabbit onto a sharp stump of broken wood extruding from the brush. The rabbit struggled to live, but it was useless. The bird swooped and returned for its prey. It tore the head and upper feet away and continued on his journey satisfied.

As Toby watched, he realized that the

brush was shaped like a cross and the rabbit was torn open and bleeding down the brush. He was reminded of his vision. He thought of all the things he and Great Pa had spoken about, and of the letters he had read sitting on the white buffalo hide as Great Pa lay dying.

Bad and evil things had come into his life since he had turned his life toward his mother's world. He couldn't stop now. He must not turn his back on God. Somewhere in that Book of His, it said, "Vengeance is mine. I will repay."

So Toby decided. The acres and cave were his. Great Pa had seen to that. It would be here when he was ready for it. Toby would go to the white man's school. He would study to be a doctor for the animals, is what Great Pa would say. It would take some time, but he would come back in the summers.

"Who knows, my heart might even return here someday, as well. Yes! This is the way it will be. The first part of my life closes and now I will see what happens in the next part."

CHAPTER 36

What first? Prepare to leave the mountain. So Toby made the cabin and the premises secure. He took down the tepee and put it in the cabin. Toby sealed the door to the cave from the inside. Then he sealed the cabin door from the outside. "Only fire will bring this down." Then he went around to the waterfall and entered the cave. He put rocks over the opening, just in case it really did burn, and then he sealed the sliding wall as best as he could. Then Toby put his mementos in a safe and dry place. "That should be secure for three or four years. I should be back by then."

Toby took one more look around. He picked up his deerskin duffle, threw it over his shoulder, and started down the mountain and out of the forest.

Once again, he turned and looked up on the forest. After a long moment, he sighed deeply and continued on the path to the Moore's place.

Mrs. Moore was busy in her garden, but Mr. Moore was sitting under a large tree near the house. He was whittling on a piece of wood. Making nothing. Just whittling and in deep reserve. He jumped when Toby spoke. "Hey, Mr. Moore. You appear to be awfully busy this morning."

"Whew! You scerred me."

"Sorry, I just came to say goodbye."

"Now, Toby, don't go and run off. Ye'll git over what happened."

"I'll never forget what happened, but I'll take care of that. However, that's not the reason I'm leaving. I'm going to go to school. That should be enough time for both Gabby and me to heal. I plan to come back and marry your daughter."

"Wal now, I'm glad to hear you say so, Toby, and I'm glad you feel thata way."

"I wrote Gabby a note to tell her my plan. Now I want you to tell her 'the same exact thing that happened to her also happened to me'. Tell her privately, please. Be sure and tell her the exact thing happened to me. She'll know!"

"I will! And good luck, son."

"I'll be on my way now. See ya."

"Yeah! Godspeed." He tucked the note for his daughter into his pocket and went inside.

Toby went on down the path to the schoolhouse. He found Mr. Macon making lesson plans for the coming week.

"Come in, Toby, come on in. Glad you came by." He noticed Toby's duffle. "What's this? Are you going somewhere?"

"That's what I came to tell you. I've decided to do what you and Great Pa wanted me to do a couple of years ago. I'm going on to school!"

Mr. Macon clapped his hands and danced around in a circle, grinning all over his face. "I'm glad. I'm so very glad. And don't the Lord just work wonders?"

"Is that who is pushing me now? I just thought it might be a good time to go. I need your help, as usual."

"Sit, let's talk. Just say what you need. I'll do what I can to help."

"Well, first of all I need papers from you so that I can get into school. Then I'll need you to call your father to prepare him for my visit to him. Maybe, since he's my lawyer, he can help me set up a way to pay as I go. A bank account or something will do. And tell him I will be there in a few days."

"Sure, I can do all of that. I'll even take you when you are ready."

"No! No! I'm going to walk for awhile. Take my time. Sleep out. I need some time alone. I thought I might stop by and say goodbye to Doc Johns."

"Sure. I understand."

From where Toby sat, he could see across the road to The Post. He saw the O'Shiras go in. "I think I'll go over to The Post. I need to say goodbye to Mr. Otson. Wanna go?"

"No, I have to finish up here. If you're still there later, I'll join you."

"Great. Mind if I leave my gear here?"

"Go ahead."

So Toby strolled into the store in his usual manner. He spoke to everyone inside. Then he approached Mr. Otson. "I came by to pay my bill if I owe you anything. Oh and would you make up an overnight bag of snacks and a canteen of water for me?"

"Hey, Toby, where ya headed? Weuns is goin' trapp'n and fishin' a little. Whonja jine up with us?" whined Clyde.

"Sorry, Clyde, I better not. I haven't been having much luck lately with my traps." He noticed how red-faced Jessie became. "Say, Mr. Otson, set the boys up with a pop and put it on my bill."

Clyde grinned, "That's good a ye, Toby, considerin'-"

The cousins interrupted Clyde with their thanks and stepped out on the porch. All but Jessie.

He moved casually nearer to Toby with his back toward the others. "Thanks for the pop. Uh, Toby, I'm sorry about the dumb stuff I've done to ya. Really, really sorry about some of the stuff I've done recently. Truly sorry," he whispered.

"Yeah, me too." Toby looked him in the eye. "Remember when we used to sit outside that church house sometime and wonder about it? Well, you should go in and listen sometime.

"Hey, come on, Jess," yelled Zeek.

Jessie nearly knocked Mr. Macon down as he ran hurriedly out of the store.

"What was that about?"

"I just invited him to go to church. What are you drinking?"

Toby got out an orange drink for Mr. Macon and they visited for awhile.

"Toby, I got your stuff together. You never did say where you'as goin'."

"Well, Mr. Otson, I'm leaving this evening, and I'm going to be making my way to Macon. I've decided to go to school. Now

I want you to keep doing business as usual. Just see Mr. Macon if there's a problem.

"Well, I'll be. That's good. And I will."

"You ready, Mr. Macon?" They left together. They went across the road back to the school. Toby stopped and turned to Mr. Macon. "What do you think about hiring some kind of law to come live on this mountain? It seems that might be a way I could look out for things while I'm gone. I'd pay his wages if I need to."

"You know, that might be a good idea. I'll get with my father and see what might need to be done. Toby, you stay in touch. I go to Macon some. I'll see you there."

"Oh, don't worry, I'm sure I'll be back some. There's the summers. I'll need to visit Mr. Otson, and I need to see Mr. Moore to keep up with Gabby." He stuck out his hand and shook hands then embraced Mr. Macon. "Thanks for being my friend." He started down the mountain to say goodbye to Doc Johns. He paused, turned to Mr. Macon, and said, "Sir, may I tell you something one Christian brother to another?"

"Of course, Toby. What is it?"

"I hope you don't think I've lost my rational thinking, but I'd like to pray."

"Toby, there is nothing crazy about

praying."

Toby knelt there outside on the path. Mr. Macon joined him. "Lord God, first I thank you for my brothers and my friends. I ask you to bless them and this place. And, God, please understand what I mean when I say thank you for what has happened to me. While I hate the act and the shame I still feel, you, God, have allowed me to walk in the moccasins of my Gabby Delight with whom I now share an understanding. Strengthen her and allow me to help in some way. And, God, please forgive my thoughts. In the name of Jesus," he paused. Toby looked at his friend with tears in his eyes and running down his face.

"Amen!" exclaimed Mr. Macon. He stood and gave a hand to Toby. As Toby slowly rose, Mr. Macon spoke again with depth, "Go now, Toby. God will answer your prayer. I've never seen such feeling in one so young. Give my best to Doc Johns."

"Yes, sir, and thank you. I owe you greatly."

"Nonsense. Godspeed."

Toby started down the mountain to the village.

CHAPTER 37

Toby meditated as he traveled to the village below.

"Samson had used the jawbone of an ass to kill hundreds of his enemies."

One never knows with whom or with what God might do His thing. He just knew that God was in charge, and his soul would not be happy if he sinned against God by giving in to his strong vengeful feelings.

He didn't, for one minute, blame God for his own decision. He would do what he felt he must do to put an end to the rampage.

Others could have done it, but no one else knew who the culprits were. He knew. Oh yes, he knew beyond doubt. He could still feel that four-fingered hand on his backside. He shuddered.

Toby had hidden in the forest after his visit with Doc Johns to await the right time to begin his plan.

The O'Shiras had been noisily spreading their hunting plans all around the village. So Toby knew where they would be. He'd been hunting with them enough to know their routine.

Toby walked quietly through the woods. He was wearing the same foot cover they had used. It was no wonder there had never been any footprints at the scene of the crimes. The woolen sheepskin pads distorted the foot's shape and left no print. Besides that, he could walk quietly through the trees.

He walked steadily along to the vet's barn secure in the fact that Doc Johns had driven to the city for a day or two. Even so, he went carefully. He must not be seen. He wasn't sure how the villagers would feel about what he had decided to do. He would act alone. As he approached the medicine bin, Ole Rose sneaked up behind and palmed her cold nose into Toby's hand. He caught his breath and sighed relief. "I'm glad it's you, ole girl," he whispered. Rose was an old friend. She wouldn't tell anyone that he'd been there.

Toby reached into the cabinet and found the chloroform and tools he would need. There would be plenty of time to clean and return the things before Doc Johns came in on Monday.

The journey through the mountain's forest would be no problem, or so he believed. Most folks stayed in on misty nights like this. That is except the hunters. Toby knew the routine. He had grown up in these mountains. He knew the people and the animals.

Up above about one hundred yards, there was a glow from their campfire. The real task lay ahead. Toby worked his way around the trees and rocks like one of the animals he loved so well. He wondered if even the animals would be less restless when this night was over.

Toby had fasted first and prayed for several hours. He was hungry, but he couldn't eat until he finished his work. He was cool as he stepped behind the large pine.

He could see all five men rolled up the way he knew they would be. Jessie was curled around the glowing coals of the fire. Clyde, ever shy of the fire, was several feet away with his back turned to the fire. Jake and Daniel were passed out at the foot of a tree just inside the fire's light. Zeek, as ever the leader, posted himself just outside the circle of light leaning against a fine, large tree.

He only appeared to be on guard. Everyone in the mountains knew he was the first to sleep. He slept upright with his eyes open.

Toby figured him to be the one to be fixed first. Toby approached cautiously. He came up on the right side of the tree. The ethered cloth in his big hand just fit Zeek's face. There was no struggle. He just went limp. Toby half drug and half carried the limp man to the spot he'd chosen to use. Toby tied him in position and went back for the second one.

One by one, Toby put them into deeper sleep and carried them to the cove of strong, young trees he had found.

Movement in the underbrush startled him once. It was some small nocturnal animal searching for food.

Toby took the razor sharp instrument from his bag and removed the cover. He had planned well. He had all he would need to bring his foolish rampage to an end. He even knew the cousins would be found and cared for.

Toby was sure he would be finished here, cleaned up, and gone when the hunters made their discovery.

He wanted to frighten these men as they had frightened their victims. He knew their cowardly hearts and blood, lots of blood, would do the trick.

He took the large jar of blood he had borrowed from Doc Johns. The Doc liked blood pudding. This would be put to a better use.

Toby put burrs that he had collected from various rape scenes between their toes. Then he covered the feet with the sheepskin booties he'd retrieved from their hunting bags. Then he poured blood on the skins. When they awakened, they'd think their feet had been cut because of the blood and the burning, along with the stinging from the burrs and needles he'd used from the forest. They'd think their feet and bodies had been cut all over. It wouldn't take long to realized where they had really been cut.

The unused blood he would return to Doc's. Poor Ole Rose would be blamed.

Toby shivered as he realized he was actually enjoying himself.

"Shame on you, Toby Singletree." He grinned and continued on his mission.

After pouring blood on the five men, he took the knife and began the task that would be a favor to the future young women who would live on this mountain. The deed was done!

He was glad he had only cut Jessie on and

around his legs. They had been friends too long and Toby believed Jessie had a good heart. Their acts of rape could not be proven. But they must be stopped. He was the stopper.

God said, "Thou shalt not kill." So he didn't kill.

He stood back and looked at his work. Five evil men hung upside down, tied, feet spread apart on handmade singletrees. The bleeding would stop soon. Toby knew that. He was good at what he did.

They reminded him of the pigs he had castrated, but they weren't squealing. Not yet anyway. As they began to awaken from the chloroform he'd administered and were yet not conscious, Toby removed all traces of his presence. Then Toby did the same act of kindness he'd always done to help stop the bleeding on the pigs. He poured a handful of salt on the open wounds. Now they were squealing!

Soon someone would come down the trail. The cousins would be discovered and lowered. They'd be sore for awhile. They might continue to be evil, but they could never rape again. If the cousins had ever found out Jessie had escaped, they would do him themselves.

Toby was as discrete as the rapists had been. He left no clue, no trail, and everyone thought he'd left the mountain two days ago.

Only God and Toby knew who had done the deed. The mountains were silent and watched. They were sure to keep their secret.

THE END

OR...

THE BEGINNING!

ABOUT THE AUTHOR

B. F. Gill is an 82-year-old retired elementary school teacher. Ms. Gill began this story after retiring in 1991. She feels she owes her students an apology for taking so long. Below is a message from her:

"After my last days of teaching, I went into mission work. I continued teaching for twenty-four years to women in Texas jails. I taught the Bible. For seven years I taught two to three months of each year at Monterrey, Mexico School of Preaching. In 2006-2007, I taught the ladies in Cochabamba, Bolivia who were or had been in jail. That is where I finished my book about Toby. To my fourth graders at Sands ISD in 1991: I'm sorry I took so long. After that, I didn't know how to publish. Several authors said they would help me, but they got busy. Oh well, 2017 isn't so late!"